MW01171181

Do The Work

An Anthology from

the Writelage Gang

of the Education Underground

Edited by Mr. C

DEDICATION

To Michelle Miles, who lent her house to us for meetings and hours of arguing and discussing and writing and editing, and never said a sour word. Also—this would never have happened without you.
You know what you did.

The Work

ACKNOWLEDGMENTS

We should acknowledge the parents, without whose financing the workshop would never have happened, and whose patience and prodding ultimately should find some of its reward in this volume.

Special thanks to Michelle Miles, whose idea this workshop was and who did more than anyone to see it come together.

And as always, thanks to Kathryn Russell, who taught me to write, and Daniela Larsen, who asked me to teach. Without them, none of this could have ever happened.

Editor's Note:

Finishing is hard work.

This is a thing most people don't really know. Everyone wants to be an author, a writer, a creator. But there's a huge difference between writing and finishing, as these kids just found out.

Starting in September 2023, eleven young people and I began some work together. Meeting in a kitchen in Lehi, UT, about a block from the old cemetery, we started a process to turn a group of aspiring writers into authors. And as they will tell you, the difference between a writer and an author is that authors finish.

The first few pages of a story are filled with fire and excitement and passion. A new idea! New characters! Cool worldbuilding! Ah, but then. Then the work begins, and the enthusiasm bogs down. The idea got us going, but it's not enough by itself. The characters have to, you know, do stuff, new stuff, all the time. The world is fun to explore, but exploration is not a story.

Getting from the first few pages to the end of the story is brutal.

I gave them an assignment: pick a story and finish it. No less than 2000 words, and no more than 12,000. I thought that would give enough scope for their imagination. It did. Sort of.

Oddly (at least to me), some of them chafed at the word limit. They wanted to write something longer. And longer is fine, as long as it gets finished.

If you don't finish, you have written. But you have not authored. The work has to be finished for it to be alive.

Finishing is excruciating. The process of getting that start to keep momentum through the mucky middle and to the satisfying conclusion is so hard that most people never make it. Most writers have drawers, thumb drives, hard drives filled with stories that didn't quite live. Starts that withered.

And that happened here, too. We don't have twelve stories (including mine). We have eleven. And a couple of them...ran out of steam. Good ideas, interesting plots, fun places, worthwhile people. Just not quite finished.

That's okay. One thing we learned was that the work has value whether it gets completed or not. But if you're going to go from writer to author, you have to finish. All of us—all of us—had to start stuff we didn't finish. And we worked through it, and we wrote until we learned to finish, and then we could get to the end of one thing, and then the next thing. Eventually, if you keep going, you can learn to finish everything you start.

But it takes work.

It takes work to learn to write a good story. It takes work to learn the rules of grammar and spelling and punctuation, so that our writing can be clear. It takes work to make your characters speak like real people (but not too much like real people), to make your world real, to make your place and problem interesting enough to keep the reader's attention.

We didn't do those things perfectly. There's a lot of clunky stuff here. There are intricate plots that did not quite intri-cate.

There are characters that speak like, um, not-quite-humans. And there are scenes that...well, you'll meet the Paris sewers soon enough. And there are one or two stories that are not...quite...finished.

But we did one thing.

We did the work.

And here it is.

Mr. C

P.S. You will likely find that the grammar here is a bit rough and the punctuation not entirely MLA style (or whatever school you favor). That's intentional. With most of these stories I opted, as editor, to preserve the original voice in the text rather than iron it out by making it fit a preset rule. If that meant—and it did—that the text demonstrates that the author has an, um, tenuous grasp of what a sentence is, so be it.

I beg your tolerance and forgiveness, dear reader.

Beyond The Fairytales

Jamie Allred

Prologue

A soft breeze drifted through the smooth silky curtains of the earthy elven castle as the full moon shone on two precious sleeping babies. They both had shiny golden-brown hair and rosy cheeks. In the corner, a dark shadowy figure watched the princesses sleep. Slowly, without making a sound, the cloaked form crept towards the crib nearest to her and gently picked up the small child. The princess stirred and whimpered as the figure slowly rocked her back and forth.

"Shhhh. Soon you will be home," the figure whispered in

a sweet smooth feminine voice. She tip-toed towards the other cradle and attempted to pick up the other baby. This twin however, was a very light sleeper. At the slightest touch she would awaken. As the woman caressed the small pudgy arm with her finger, the princess abruptly started crying. Sounds from the hallway. The nurse was coming. The kidnapper knew she could not be discovered here. Having no choice, the woman left the second child and hurried to the window. Quickly, she slipped the baby into a knapsack that was slung over her shoulder before she scrambled down a rope ladder and disappeared into the mist.

Chapter One

Holly

I stood up and wiped beads of sweat off my forehead as I gazed to the West, careful not to look directly at the sun which was barely brushing the fiery mountains. The mountains were gorgeous. Even the nastiest person alive couldn't argue about that. It was like a painting, painted so perfectly, every detail demanded attention. Streaks of blue, purple, pink, yellow and orange lit up the sky. The tips of the mountains were crowned with a blanket of snow which reflected a light coral hue against the myriad of colors. I turned my head to the north and frowned at the line of honking cars on the freeway that ruined the fairytale-like scene.

"Holly May Andersen, I told you to have this area weeded

before it's time for dinner and here I find you just standing there, staring at nothing."

I whirled around and faced my mother. By anybody's standards, she was very attractive. Her blonde, almost white hair was naturally wavy and her pale blue eyes were like two crystal pools. Her red lips were pressed into a tight line revealing a small dimple on her cheek.

Unfortunately, I didn't look anything like her. I had dirty-blonde hair that was almost brown and had the slightest tint of auburn if the sun hit it at a certain angle. My eyes were blue as well but they were a completely different shade. I wasn't ugly but I certainly wasn't as gorgeous as my mother.

"I'm sorry, I was just looking at the sunset." I looked at my feet. My mom laughed.

"I was teasing. You think I would get mad at you on your birthday?" She smiled.

"I never know what you'll do." I muttered so she couldn't hear. I didn't know why I was feeling bitter toward my mother lately. It might've been because she was always changing her mind about things or being way too....secretive? I couldn't describe it, but whatever it was, I didn't like it. Not one bit.

"Well, come inside. Your sister and I have a surprise for you after dinner," Mom said over her shoulder as she walked towards the house. I narrowed my eyes at those perfect curls as they bounced lightly on my mother's shoulders. They seemed to mock me. Laugh at me.

Reluctantly, I followed her into the house.

— — — * — — —

I set down my fork and leaned back in my chair, too full to eat another bite. Spaghetti and meatballs was my favorite meal and despite my mom's recent strange behavior, she was still an amazing cook.

"How was it?" my mom asked.

"Delicious, thanks."

My six-year-old sister, Claire, agreed as she crammed the last few noodles into her mouth.

"Good. Now, come into the garage. I have a surprise for you!"

"Is it a surprise for me too?" Claire asked hopefully as she jumped down from her seat next to mine.

Mom rolled her eyes in annoyance. "No, Claire. Is it your birthday?"

Claire scrunched her nose, "I don't think–"

Mom interrupted her and shouted, "Then why would you get a present!"

Claire jumped. "I-I-I'm sorry."

I gaped. Was my mom crazy? She NEVER yelled at Claire. No one did. She was the sweetest thing on planet earth. I watched closely as something in my mom's eyes changed. What was it? Shock? Did she look. . .guilty?

"I'm sorry, Claire, I've just been out of it ever since my sister died last week." She opened the door. I had forgotten that my aunt had died recently. I had never met her. I had never seen any of my relatives except one time I vaguely remembered seeing my grandpa, but I was too little to remember much. He had been in a fight with my mother. I can't remember what it was about. I do remember his smell though. He smelled of pumpkin spice and cloves. He was kind to me.

My mom looked back at me. "Do you want your present or not?" Still staring, I followed her into the garage. In the corner, sitting on a small white table with an orange tablecloth, was a brown paper bag.

"Are you going to open it?" My mom asked, pointing to the bag. Slowly I walked to the table and picked it up. I reached my hand inside and pulled out a plain gold chain with a small heart shaped charm. I smiled as I put the bracelet on my wrist.

"Thank you," I said. "I love it," my mom was about to reply when her cell phone rang. Her face somehow turned green and red when she saw her caller. Before me or my sister could say a word she had hurried in the house and disappeared inside her room.

Unsure what to do I led my sister to the kitchen to get a drink of water. Several minutes later, my mom came out, looking very pale.

"Mom," I said. "Are you ok?"

She blinked. "Come into the living room. There's something I need to tell you. I'll be there in a second". Curious, I walked into the family room where my dad was watching the news on the couch.

"Hi, dad," I said as I sat next to him. He only gave me a blank stare. A year after I was born he had been in a bad car accident and couldn't talk or remember anyone very well. Sometimes I would see him stare at my mom or whisper her name. I didn't understand why he only seemed to remember her. Something that puzzled me though, was that, whenever he said my mom's name, he said it with hatred and whenever he looked at her, he seemed to glare at her. I kept telling myself it was just the effects of the accident but deep down I knew it was something else.

I glanced down at the empty food tray on his lap. Thankfully for my mom, he could still care for himself. My mom came into the living room and stood in front of the TV, muting it so it wouldn't be a distraction.

"Girls," she began. "The city is being shut down. There have been several sightings of Gundumbols." I glanced out the window, looking around for any sign of one. From what I had heard they had orange hair all over their body and were shaped roughly like a dwarf. They had purple tusks that protruded from a scabby mouth. And they could manipulate anyone that stared into their eyes for longer than ten seconds. I shivered. I did *not* want to see one. I don't know exactly why, but I had a weird feeling that my mom wasn't being completely honest.

"Is anyone being controlled right now?" I asked after a moment, deciding to play along.

"Not that we know of." She took a deep breath. My mom was a member of the city council so she knew all about what was happening. "Anyways, school is canceled and the grocery stores are being shut down. Special scouts will deliver groceries to our door." Again I knew she was not telling the truth.

"Where did they come from?" Claire asked.

My mom hesitated and bit her lip, "Ummm, no one knows." Why was my mom lying? And why was she acting so nervous? I would just have to wait and see.

Chapter Two

Lucy

August 31, 2023

Dear Journal,

My name is Lucy Hayfield. My birthday is today and I turned fifteen. My Uncle gave me this journal and said I should start writing in it. I guess I should have started one earlier in my life but I just never got to it. Anyway, I live with my Aunt Jane and Uncle Liam. My mom died in childbirth and I don't know where my dad is. Aunt Jane and Uncle Liam are really nice. I think of them as my parents. They have two kids, a girl aged fourteen and a boy who is almost thirteen. We recently moved to Idaho. I don't know why we moved, our new house is quite small and our old house was perfectly fine. Well *it's almost time for dinner. Bye!*

Lucy Hayfield

I leaned back in my chair to look at my first journal entry but all I could focus on was "I turned fifteen." Was I really fifteen? It seemed like yesterday I turned fourteen. Has it really been a year? I sighed and stared out at the sunset. It was gorgeous. This was one thing I *did* like about Idaho. Our old house didn't have this breathtaking view.

"Lucy, it's time for dinner." I jumped in my seat as Victoria walked into the room, weaving through boxes to get to me. She looked over my shoulder at my journal.

"How do you like your journal?"

"I love it! I wish I had started it a few years ago though.," I said.

My cousin nodded. "Well, anyway we are having Alfredo for dinner."

My stomach growled. I loved Alfredo and my aunt always made it perfectly. I stood up and rushed down the stairs. I breathed in the delicious scent as Victoria descended the stairs behind me. I sprinted to the kitchen where Aunt Jane was placing the food on the table. Victoria and I sat down at the table. Aunt Jane looked up.

"Happy birthday, sweetheart," she said, coming around to me and kissing me on the cheek. I breathed in her scent. She smelled like fall. Pumpkin spice and cloves. Cinnamon and ginger. Fall was my favorite season because of her. "Now, I'm hungry. Victoria, go get your father and brother so we can eat."

Victoria sighed. "Fine." She reluctantly got up from the table and slipped out the front door. Aunt Jane disappeared into the back room and came out a moment later with a small square box, wrapped in white wrapping paper with pink and yellow polka-dots. A big turquoise bow almost covered the entire top of the box. She placed it in the center of the table.

"Can I open it?" I asked.

My aunt laughed. "Nope."

"You put it there just to torture me, didn't you?" I pouted. My aunt was about to answer when Victoria came through the door followed by a middle-aged man with dark hair and blue eyes, and a boy almost identical to his father. Both were dripping wet.

I gasped.

"Where have you two been?" Aunt Jane said. She put her hands on her hips.

Uncle Liam and Lucas grinned at each other. "Dad pushed me in the pool," Lucas finally said.

"Only after you sprayed me with the hose!" Uncle Liam retorted.

"I sprayed you with the hose because you poured a bucket of water on my head!" Lucas fired back.

"I–"

"Enough!" Aunt Jane interrupted. Everyone froze. "You have two minutes to change your clothes before I make you both have cold showers for the rest of the week!" Uncle Liam and Lucas hurried upstairs, like dogs with their tails between their legs.

I glanced at my aunt, which was a mistake. Her face was almost purple from trying not to laugh. One look at her and I had had it. I burst out laughing. It caused a chain reaction and my aunt and cousin began giggling too. When the laughing finally subsided I clutched my stomach.

"I have never seen them so scared!" Victoria said.

"They were terrified!" I managed to say.

"Shh. Here they come," Aunt Jane said. We tried to look bored as Lucas and Uncle Liam walked into the kitchen. They had fresh clothes on and their hair was nicely combed though it was still wet.

"Now, are we ready to eat?" Aunt Jane asked with mock innocence. Uncle Liam ignored her and turned his attention to me.

"How was your birthday?" he asked.

"Good."

"Do you like your journal?"

I nodded enthusiastically. My Uncle smiled.

"Alfredo, huh?" Lucas asked as he settled into his seat.

"It's Lucy's favorite." Victoria said. "Mine too."

"Well, let's dig in," Aunt Jane said.

— — — * — — —

After dinner we gathered in the living room. I sat down in a large lounge chair and tucked my feet in under myself. The others sat across from me on a gray couch that still had a plastic covering from the moving van. My aunt took a deep breath.

"Where should I start?" she said to herself. "Have you heard of the Wilder Twins?" she asked me and the others. We all shook our heads. "Well, they were born fifteen years ago. Their mother was said to possess magic powers. Unfortunately, she died while giving birth to the twins. The twins were like mirrors to each other. No one could tell the difference between them. Except their eyes. One baby had blue eyes while the other had emerald green. The twins had no relatives except for one Aunt. So they went to live with her. When the twins were three months old one of them got kidnapped. People thought that the twins inherited their mother's magic or powers or whatever you want to call it. After one of the twins was kidnapped, the aunt took the other one and went into hiding to protect her. And no one has ever heard of them since."

She seemed to be telling the story only to me. And then I got it.

"You're my aunt," I said.

"I am."

"And the twin that disappeared with her aunt is...me?" I said.

Aunt Jane nodded. "You are one of the twins, yes."

"I have a twin?" I couldn't believe it. I had a twin!

"Yes." Aunt Jane went to the kitchen and came out with the gift. "Do you want to open your present now?"

Too scared to speak, I nodded. She handed me the box and I slowly pulled off the paper. Inside was a cardboard box. I peeled away the sides and pulled out a white envelope with the name *Savanna* written in beautiful cursive.

I glanced questioningly at my aunt. "Savanna?" I asked. She motioned for me to open it. I tore open the seal and pulled out a piece of paper. The writing on it was old and worn but still readable.

Dear Savanna,

Happy birthday, Savanna. I have asked your aunt to give this letter to you when you turn fifteen. This is your mother. I am writing this letter about a week before you and your sister are expected to be born. Most elves die while giving birth to twins and I am no different. I am not expecting to live. Oh how I wish I could see you and your sister grow up. Who knows, maybe I will.

By now you probably know that I have been said to have magical powers. That is true. In case you do not know, you are a princess, a half-elf princess. I am an elf and your dad is a human. You are the heir to the throne. In time you will take responsibility.

The elves have been hiding. Without a queen they do not feel safe. You need to prove to them that you are the queen's daughter. Some think that one or both of you have inherited these powers. That is also true. I could feel it before you were born. In time you will discover what these powers are. I can not tell you for your safety. Know that I love you and your sister very much. Be careful and be safe. There are many people who would like to take these gifts from you. I wish I could have spent my life with you.

Love,

Mother

I sat back in my seat, too overwhelmed to say anything. My mind felt muddy as I tried to process the letter and everything my aunt told me.

"May I read it?" Aunt Jane asked. I handed her the note. She took it and began to read. I glanced at Victoria who was looking at me. Puzzlement painted her face. I couldn't process what she wanted me to do. Little black dots blurred my vision. It was like looking down a pipe. The hole grew smaller and smaller until everything went black.

_ _ _ * _ _ _

"Lucy?" I moaned and slowly sat up. Had I just fainted? I never fainted. I was lying on the couch. My aunt sat at the end of the couch rubbing my feet. Victoria, Lucas and Uncle Liam all crowded around me.

"How long was I out?" I asked.

"Eight minutes," Victoria said.

"I suspected you would faint," Aunt Jane said. "Quite a bit of news. Do you feel okay?"

"I'm fine. Just a little woozy." I paused. "My name is Savanna?" Aunt Jane nodded. "What's my sister's name?"

"Her name is Sierra."

Savanna and Sierra Wilder. I tried the names on my tongue.

"But she thinks her name is Holly Andersen," Uncle Liam said.

"Wait, how do you know that?" I demanded. "You all knew about this?"

"I didn't," muttered Victoria.

Aunt Jane took a deep breath. "Do you know why we moved here?"

"No." I held my breath.

"Well, one of my friends was here on a trip and they saw a girl that looked just like you. They tried to talk to her, thinking it was you, but she bolted and they lost her in a big grocery store. We were hoping you would help look for her and if she got any of her mother's personality, she won't be able to stay away."

"You want *me* to look for her?!" I exclaimed. When my aunt nodded I sat back in my chair and processed the additional news. *More news.* This was the craziest day of my life. "Okay, what if I just find out her address and send her a letter?"

"She was kidnapped. She knows nothing about this. Chances are she will reject it. I don't think a letter is the way to go here."

"What if I see her at school, or somewhere, or what if someone comes up to me and they 'know me' but I don't know them?" I asked.

"Just act like you know what's going on," Uncle Liam said. "We might get information that way."

"Okay," I said after a moment. "Okay."

"We've worked hard to find your sister. I think her 'mom' suspects we are looking for her and we think she is here." Uncle Liam paused, "If only we knew where she was."

Aunt Jane sighed. "Poor girl."

No kidding. I couldn't imagine being lied to my whole life. Strike that. I knew *exactly* how that felt, but I could understand why they didn't tell me earlier. I wondered what Sierra was doing right now.

Holly

I stared up at the ceiling, seeing nothing. A small sliver of moonlight penetrated the blackness. The quiet snoring of Claire broke the silence. I had always shared a room with my sister and frankly, I didn't mind it. It was someone to keep me company.

I only had one friend. I had known Avery for as long as I could remember. She was always there for me. I shifted onto my side and hugged my pillow, squeezing my eyes shut to hold back the tears. That is, she was always there before she moved away. Now all I had was my sister and my dad. My mom didn't seem to care about us. I knew deep down she did, but she rarely showed it. I felt guilty feeling sorry for myself but I couldn't help it. I needed *someone* to feel sorry for me.

Trying to remove my mind from my life problems, I thought about galloping away on my horse. Her sleek ebony coat shone like a thousand stars. My horse, Raven, had a secret. She was invincible. I still couldn't figure out why, but I was determined to find out one day.

Eventually, I drifted off to sleep.

Lucy—one week later

"Aunt Jane," I began as I finished spreading cream cheese on my perfectly toasted plain bagel, "Do you think Holly has a phone?"

"I assume so. Unfortunately, it's hard to find a teenager without a phone these days."

"I'll probably see if I can look her up on Instagram or

something." I placed my beautifully made bagel on a plate and filled in the empty space with strawberries, blackberries and raspberries. I carried it to the table and sat down next to Lucas.

"Hey," I said.

"Hello your majesty."

I rolled my eyes. "Please don't call me that."

"You're so weird. If I were a prince, I would insist people call me your highness, great lord, your majesty, your excellency, etcetera etcetera. And I would command them to do everything for me, make my bed, clean my room, do all my jobs, take me anywhere I want, give me money, you get the gist of it." My cousin shoved a spoonful of cocoa puffs into his mouth.

"Oh, so you want to be a tyrant?"

"Of course."

"Would you want to be *ruled* by a tyrant?"

He hesitated. "I guess not."

I smiled and took a bite of my bagel. Delicious. I pulled out my phone, opened Instagram and typed in the name 'Holly Andersen.' There were a lot of them. Hundreds, it seemed like. But it wasn't hard to find who I was looking for because I knew exactly what she looked like. Luckily she had a profile picture of her face. I was shocked how much she actually did look like me. Just her eyes were different. I clicked on her account and scrolled through the pictures. One picture in particular caught my attention. It was a selfie of her and another little girl with dark brown curls and green eyes. The scene behind them looked familiar, but I couldn't quite place it.

"Whoa. Is that Sierra? She looks exactly like you." Victoria said over my shoulder. In her hand she carried a half-eaten piece of toast with strawberry jam.

"Let me see," Lucas said, leaning over to look at the picture, "Isn't that the park we went to when we first moved here?"

"Ohhhhh. I remember now. It's only a few blocks away, right?" I said.

"I think so," Victoria said.

"She probably doesn't live too far away then,"

"Probably." Lucas stood up to clear his bowl as I finished up my bagel and fruit. I carried my plate to the sink and rinsed it off before walking to the family room and sinking down onto the couch. I continued to look at Holly's posts. I found out that her mom, Marinda Andersen, was a trained therapist. I tried to look her up on Instagram but with no luck. Facebook was also a dead end. Why couldn't I find her? I looked all over social media but found no trace of her except for Sierra's comments about her 'mother'.

"Did you find anything?" Aunt Jane asked from the doorway.

"Yes."

Aunt Jane came to sit beside me and I showed her the few pictures I had found. There were only two that really stood out to me. There was the picture of her at the park, and a selfie of her making a "shhh" sign in front of her mouth and pointing with the other hand at her mom interviewing a patient in an office. Below the picture of her mom small words said, 'the most amazing therapist in the world!' It said it had been posted two years ago.

"So her mom's a therapist?" my aunt said,

"I think so."

"Did you search up her name?"

"I tried everywhere I could. There was no trace of her."

"Interesting. How does she get clients?"

"Very weird." I agreed. "What should we do?"

Aunt Jane sighed. "Okay, well, we know she probably lives close, right? Because of the park picture."

"Guess it's time to take a walk in the park."

Holly—two weeks later

I had to get out of the house. I had been stuck here for three weeks and I had to get out. I was getting claustrophobic. Because my mom had an actual important job, she was allowed to leave. Claire went with her today because she was sick and my mom wanted to keep an eye on her, which was weird. She never did that. But then again, lately, my mom has not been acting naturally.

I didn't actually believe there were gundumbols everywhere, but I didn't understand why my mom would make up something like that. What was she trying to do? It probably had to do with the way she was behaving.

I glanced at my watch. It read 12:26. I hurriedly finished making a ham sandwich for my dad. I set the sandwich on a plate and carried it to the family room where he sat on the couch with a picture book of 'Curious George.'

"Hi Dad," I said, placing the plate of food on his lap. He

made no move to eat it, but that was normal. He usually didn't start eating until he was alone. I stepped out of the room and made up my mind to go outside. I grabbed my shoes and a light sweater before slipping out the front door. My eyes filled with tears as I breathed in the fresh scent of fall. The scent I had missed for so long.

_ _ _ * _ _ _

I don't know why I decided to go to the park. Maybe it was because I wanted to see the joy on the children's flushed faces as they ran around laughing and smiling. I half expected the playground to be vacant, but it was as busy as ever. I walked over to the swings and began pumping my legs to gain momentum. Soon, I felt like I was in the clouds. I tipped my head back and closed my eyes. The wind weaved through my hair as I went back and forth, back and forth. I didn't want this moment to end. But, I had to let another little kid have a turn. I opened my eyes and began slowing down when something or should I say *someone* caught my eye. A sight so eerie and terrifying I literally fell off the swing. A plump mother nearby saw the clumsy act and came rushing over to help me.

"Are you okay?" she asked.

I stood up and brushed myself off. "Yes. Thank you."

"Do you need anything?"

I wanted to laugh. She was so worried over a small fall. "No, I'm fine."

"Are you sure?"

"I'm okay." Suddenly a surge of longing pierced my heart. Was this what it was like to have a mother who loved you? Who genuinely cared about you?

A toddler tugged on the woman's shirt, trying to lead her toward the slide. She smiled back at me before heeding the child's commands.

I turned my head back to the person I had seen, hoping she was still there. She was, but this time, she was looking right back at me. We gaped at each other. We looked exactly the same. Identical.

She started walking toward me. She didn't look as surprised as I felt. Like she was expecting it. Was she? I thought about turning around and running away, but my curiosity won. As she approached, I noticed that her eyes were green, not blue like mine.

"Who are you?" I said.

"My name is Lucy."

"Why do you look exactly like me?"

"Is your name Holly?"

I gawked. "How do you know my name? Who are you?"

Lucy sighed. "Where should I start? Oh, well. I guess I'll start from the beginning."

I stared open-mouthed as she explained everything. I felt like my life was turning upside down. Suddenly I had a twin? By the time she got to the part about us being elvin royalty I was sitting on the ground. And the worst part was? I believed every bit of it. I knew she was telling the truth.

"Sooo, you've been looking for me for three weeks?"

"Yep. I found you on Instagram and saw a picture you posted at the park and we've been here everyday for the last two weeks. We didn't know where else to look and this is the most popular park around. I don't expect you to believe all this, but-"

"I do. I believe you. I know when people are telling the truth."

"Oh. you do? That's cool."

"This is all too crazy. My whole life I knew I had been lied to and now? I just don't know what to do."

"I'm so sorry."

"What do we do if I decide to go with you guys?" I knew deep down I would go with them.

"Sierra -"

"Could you call me Holly? I am so used to Holly that it will take a long time to change it."

"Fair. Anyways, you have to come with us! We need to gather the elves back together. Don't you *want* to come with us?"

I let that hang in the air for a moment before I answered, "Yes, I just . . . I already have a life here and it will be hard to completely change everything."

"Oh."

"But, I guess I have too."

"Yeah, you kinda do. And don't you want to see some of your actual blood relatives?"

"I guess so. Do we have to leave right now?"

"We should probably leave as soon as possible. I advise you not to go home first. We should get away from here as soon as possible."

I took a deep breath. "Okay. What about my sister?"'

"You have a sister?"

"Yes, well, I thought she was my sister. She's six."

"Ummm, is she home?"

"No, she's at work with my mom."

"We'll have to ask my aunt about it, but we should probably get going."

Chapter Three

Holly—two weeks later

The next two weeks went fine other than the fact that I missed my sister a ton. I missed her tight brown curls. The dimple in her left cheek when she smiled. And her spunk. Oh, how I missed her spunk. Several nights I would cry myself to sleep because I missed her so much.

"How's it going?" Victoria startled me as she entered the room us three girls shared.

"It's going," I replied.

"I'm sorry you have to go through all this."

"It's fine. I just wish I could see my sister one last time," I pressed my eyes shut to block the tears.

"I'm so sorry. I can't imagine how you feel," Victoria grabbed my hands and pulled me up from the twisty chair I had been sitting on. At least I knew they were telling the truth about all this. I would never have gone with them if I wasn't certain. Sometimes it's hard though, when someone gives you a compliment, knowing if it's true or not.

Victoria scanned the room. "We need to finish packing."

_ _ _ * _ _ _

That night I gazed out the bedroom window. The moon was full. I wondered if Claire was looking at it too. It comforted me to know that this was the same moon that shone above her. I felt closer to her. I had never been more grateful for the moon.

Suddenly I had the weird sensation that I was floating toward it. I quickly gripped the bedpost to make sure I wasn't actually floating. I couldn't tear my eyes away. It was like a magnet. It just drew me in. Then it rippled. The moon actually rippled like it was made of water. The ripples smoothed out and hardened. I narrowed my eyes. It wasn't back to its original color. It was clear. Like glass. It didn't look bumpy either. It appeared smooth. I gasped. I could see through it. I could see the stars behind it! I almost screamed at what I saw next. I could see the earth. It was like a giant mirror. I could see myself sitting on my sleeping bag. Tears leaked from my eyes. I could see Claire. She was crying on my bed. She missed me too. I had to stop this. Whatever it was, I HAD TO STOP IT! This was unbelievable. It was impossible! This couldn't be happening! Where was the "off button?" the "off switch"?!! Why had this never happened to me before?

I screamed at the top of my lungs. Lucy and Victoria bolted upright beside me. Seconds later, Aunt Jane and Uncle

Liam rushed into the room followed by Lucas.

"Holly?" Lucy asked, "What's wrong?"

"Are you okay?" Uncle Liam sat down beside me.

"What happened?" Aunt Jane grabbed my shoulders. I shook my head, clearing my thoughts.

"Just a bad dream I guess," I lied, "I'm fine."

"Are you sure?" Uncle Liam asked. I nodded.

"Do you need anything?" Aunt Jane asked.

"No." They stayed with me a few more minutes to make sure everything was really okay.

"Holly, what really happened?" Lucy asked after they left.

"How do you know it wasn't a dream?" I asked, confused.

"I don't know. I just. . . know." She scrunched up her nose.

"Ummm, I don't really know what happened. I was just looking at the moon and I could see things."

"Like what?" Victoria breathed.

"Well, I could see my sister, Claire," I said slowly.

"That's so weird. Can you do it again?" Lucy asked.

"I don't know. I don't really want to," I shuddered.

"Can you try?" Victoria asked, "But if you really don't want to, that's fine," she added quickly.

"I guess I can try.," I took a deep breath. I tried to remember how I did it. I stared at the moon. After a moment I had the same sensation. I was moving toward it. The moon rippled. When it hardened, I saw someone I had never met before. A boy, about fifteen or sixteen. He was the cutest boy I ever saw. He had brown eyes. The clearest brown I ever saw and dark brown hair. Like chocolate. He had a very defined face. He wasn't particularly tall, but not short. I wondered who this boy was. Why was I seeing him? Who was he? Was he even real? Then it was all over. The moon went back to normal. It took me a minute to realize Lucy and Victoria were still there. They looked at me expectantly.

"Did it work?" Victoria asked.

"Yes," I said slowly.

"What did you see?" Lucy asked.

"I saw a boy. I've never seen him before."

"What did he look like?" Victoria asked.

"Dark eyes and dark hair. Not very tall, but not short."

"How old did he look?" Lucy asked.

"About our age. Maybe a year older."

"Did he look cool?" We all jumped as Lucas appeared in the doorway.

"What are you doing here?" Victoria asked.

"Nothing."

"Can you please go out? We are trying to have a conversation here."

"Fine, whatever." Frustrated, Lucas left the room.

Victoria turned back to me, "Keep going."

"Anyways," I started, "I don't know why I saw him. Maybe it was just my imagination."

"I don't think you just thought that up," Lucy put in. "I think you saw him for a reason."

"Same," Victoria agreed. "Are you going to tell my mom?"

"Probably not. I don't know," I answered, "Well, we should probably get some sleep," I suggested. I didn't want to talk about this anymore. Lucy and Victoria both agreed and we settled back into our sleeping bags. That night I dreamed of Raven and me, galloping away to escape all my problems.

Chapter Four

Lucy

"Hey, Holly!" I cried the next morning. It was ten-fifteen and Holly had only just come downstairs. Her golden-brown hair was in a high messy bun and cheeks were rosy. She was wearing a baggy t-shirt and sweatpants. Even though she had just woken up, she still looked pretty. She always did. I guess that means I always look pretty, but I don't think we are as identical as people think.

"What are we having for breakfast?" She yawned.

I laughed, "You mean, 'what *did* we have for breakfast." She stared blankly at me. I smiled as realization slowly registered in her eyes.

"What time is it?"

"Almost ten thirty," her eyes widened, "Aunt Lucy saved some cinnamon pancakes for you. They are in the microwave. You might have to warm them up. We didn't want to wake you with what happened last night."

"Thanks." I was about to reply when the doorbell rang.

"It's probably the movers," I said as Holly followed me

to the door. As I opened it, Holly gasped. There were three men standing on the porch. Well, two men and a teenage boy. Holly was staring at him. He had dark hair and dark eyes. Immediately I knew who he was. This was the boy Holly had seen last night. The other two men were probably in their late thirties or early forties. They were obviously brothers and I guessed one of them was the father of the boy. They all had the same features. Dark hair and dark eyes. One of the men had a more distinct jaw and nose and was a few inches taller than the other.

"Hello, do the Hayfields live here?" the shorter one asked. His voice was deep and gravely. It was pleasant to listen to.

"Yes, are you the moving people?" I gently nudged Holly with my foot to remind her that her mouth was still almost touching the floor. Quickly, she snapped her jaw shut.

The tall man laughed. "Yes, we are the 'moving people.'" Just then Uncle Liam appeared beside me. Holly quickly slipped away. I followed her as Uncle Liam began to give them instructions. I followed Holly upstairs into our bedroom and shut the door behind me.

"Was that him?" I asked as I sat down on the floor. Holly nodded as she began to take out her hair and brush it. She still seemed to be in a daze.

"I can't believe he's a real person. I can't believe I saw him in the MOON. Like, when does a perfectly normal person see the future?"

"Holly, you have to remember you're not just a normal

person. You're a princess. An *ELF* princess."

"I guess. But so are you, and you're not seeing visions. I mean...are you?"

I shook my head.

Holly nodded. "I wonder what our home looks like. Our Elven home."

"I think it's going to be beautiful. Luscious green grass. Big trees. Gorgeous gardens."

"Oh, I hope so." She walked to the suitcase in the corner and began rummaging around for some clean clothes. I turned around to give her some privacy as she began changing into a pair of dark gray jeans and seafoam colored shirt. "Soooo, since we are elves, does that mean we will get pointy ears?"

"I don't know. I'll have to ask Aunt Jane. It's so funny. I thought I just lived a normal life, but now?" I took a breath, "I mean, I had never even really seen magical creatures but little did I know, I AM one!"

"I wonder how many people we see around are actually elves. Didn't Aunt Jane say the elves scattered or something after our mom died? Maybe we see elves every day but we don't know because they look just like humans!"

"I never thought of that, but, I guess you're right." Suddenly I had the suspicion that we were being watched. Or that someone was eavesdropping on us. Carefully I tiptoed to the door. I motioned for Holly to keep talking so the person listening wouldn't get suspicious. *If* there was someone listening. Holly began talking about something. I honestly didn't care to listen to what she was saying. I just wanted to catch whoever was spying. I waited before Holly was finished changing before I quickly threw open the door. I was surprised to see who was there. It was the last person I would expect. He gave a short gasp as he realized he'd been caught red handed.

"What were you doing?" I asked.

"I-I was just taking these boxes out to the van," the teenage boy said, motioning to the boxes by his feet. Holly came and stood next to me. She narrowed her eyes at him.

"He's lying," she said.

"How do you know?" I asked.

"I'll tell you later," She turned back to the boy. "What were you really doing?"

"Alright, can we go outside? It's really hot up here."

I glanced hesitantly at Holly. We weren't supposed to go outside because Holly's face was all over the news since she had gone 'missing.' Holly shrugged and shook her head. "Nope, sorry."

"Ugh, fine," he walked back out to the hall which was definitely cooler than our bedroom, not to mention the fact that we all would feel pretty uncomfortable if we would have been in the bedroom.

"What are your names?" The boy asked.

"I'm Lucy."

"Holly."

"Nice, my name's Calvin,"

"So, what were you doing outside of our bedroom door?" I asked.

Calvin released a long breath. "I was just walking past your door and I heard you talking about elf princesses or something. Are you guys really princesses? Wait. Are you guys the *Wilder twins*?" His eyes grew wide. Holly's mouth dropped.

"How do you know about us?" I said after a moment.

"How come you guys are together? I thought one of you got kidnapped."

"I did," Holly said, "They found me a few weeks ago."

"So you guys don't really know each other?"

"Well, we've been asking each other a bunch of 'get to know you' questions." I said.

"Oh."

"That still doesn't explain how you know about us." Holly said.

"Okay, I'll start from the beginning. My dad told me about you guys. He said your mom died when you were born and your aunt took you into hiding when Holly got kidnapped. He said one day we will find you and you guys will gather the elven kingdom again. My dad was your mom's personal guard. Your mom told my dad that his first son would become the personal guard of the oldest twin."

"WHAT? You're my personal guard?" I shouted in unbelief, "Are you an elf?"

"Yes." He suddenly became very interested in his feet

"He's telling the truth." Holly said slowly.

"Okay, how do you know?"

"I don't know, I just *know* if people are lying or telling the truth. I think it's a 'princess' thing."

"I can't," I said. Why did *she* get all the gifts? Wasn't I supposed to get the magic?

"Oh, well, I'm *positive* you'll get other things."

"Okay." I turned back to Calvin. "Keep going."

"Anyways, I've been training ever since I was six. My dad told me that when we find you guys, I'm supposed to stick with you," Calvin said.

"This is so weird," I didn't know what to think! I had my own *personal guard?* "So, I can order you around?"

"Yep. What do you want me to call you? Your Majesty? Your Highness?"

"Oh, Lucy is fine." I said hurriedly. I did not want someone following me around calling me "Your Highness."

"Well, we'd better go tell my dad," Calvin began walking inside. I still couldn't process the fact that I had a *guard.* I guess I should have expected it because I'm the princess, but still. I had only figured out that I am an elf\human a few weeks ago! My life was turning upside down.

Chapter Five

Holly—one week later

I stared out the window at the thousands of tiny cars, trampolines, houses, restaurants and stores. I had never been on an airplane before. Everyone else in our group had so they kindly let me have the window seat. It was so weird to see the world from a completely different view. I ran my hands through my now bright blonde hair. Lucy and I had dyed our hair and put in blue eye contacts to try to disguise ourselves so no one would recognize us.

We had decided to rent a hotel in Florida until we got everything figured out. I didn't exactly know what Lucy and I were supposed to do. Something about taking back the elven kingdom? I don't know.

The whole human world didn't really know anything about mythical creatures. Several years ago, before I was born, there had been a war between humans and magical creatures. The humans had won and ever since then all magic had seemed to disappear.

Every once in a while there would be rare sightings of a fairy or a gundumbol. I didn't know what mythical creatures were real and what were myths. All I knew was that I was suddenly a part of the magic. I *had* magic.

But what confused me was that only *Lucy* was supposed to have the magic, not me as well. She was the heir to the throne. I knew she did have magic. Every time I looked into her eyes I saw something that was bursting to come out. That was waiting to be discovered. I wanted to tell her because I knew she was confused about why I had magic and she didn't seem to, but I knew that she had to figure it out herself. I rubbed my eyes and yawned. I was so tired. We left our hotel in Utah at 3:30 am. And the night before we had stayed up till eleven talking about this and that. I decided to rest my eyes for a second and somehow I drifted off to sleep because the next thing I knew, Victoria was shaking me awake.

"Holly, it's time to get off. I honestly don't know how

you slept through the descent."

I rubbed my eyes and stood up. As we followed everyone off the plane, my foot caught on something and I stumbled forward but before I hit the ground, a strong hand grabbed my arm.

"Are you okay?" Calvin asked as he helped me regain my balance. I could feel my cheeks redden as I stared at my feet. I nodded.

"Thanks," I said.

"You're welcome." It had been decided that Calvin would come with us to Florida where he would finish his training and keep an eye on Lucy at the same time.

I walked a little bit faster to catch up to Victoria and escape the humiliation I was suffering.

"You look so different with your hair dyed," Victoria said, "I wouldn't be able to tell the difference between you and Lucy if you two weren't wearing different clothes."

"Do we really look that alike?" I asked. Victoria nodded enthusiastically. I fanned myself with a piece of paper that I held in my hand which I had been doodling on. Palm trees were everywhere. Big tall buildings, shops, restaurants and malls lined the streets. But the heat? I was not used to the heat. I had lived in Idaho my whole life and Florida was nothing like it.

"Is there an AC where we're staying?" Lucas asked.

Aunt Jane laughed. "Yes."

"Good. Is there a drinking fountain somewhere?"

"Yes, let's go find it. I think we could all use a drink." Uncle Liam said, "Then, let's go see our hotel."

"Well, this is it!" Uncle Liam said as he unlocked the hotel room. Victoria pushed open the door and walked in. Aunt Jane, Lucy, Victoria and I looked around the small room as Uncle Liam unlocked the room for the boys right across the hall. The only furnishings visible were two queen-sized beds, two small nightstands, a TV and a few other minor things. Fancy decorations lined shelves and sat upon desks.

"This is a nice hotel," Lucy said as she examined a small glass horse figurine.

"Yes. People pay lots of money to stay in this hotel." Aunt Jane said.

"I wonder how much stuff gets stolen," I said as I set my suitcase on the ground by the bed.

"There is nothing in this hotel that is very valuable. Besides, this particular hotel has an amazing security system," Aunt Jane said.

"How much did it cost to stay here?" Victoria asked.

"As it turns out, Jack and I are very good friends with the owner. We were able to get a major discount."

"Sooo, why exactly are we here?" Victoria said.

"We're just here until I hear back from the elf who is currently running Elixia."

"I thought all the elves were scattered?" I said.

"Yes, well, most of the elves decided to leave because they thought that you two were killed after you disappeared. They did not think they were safe unless they had a queen or king as a leader. Some of them, however, believed that you were still alive and decided to wait for your return. So there is still a small gathering of elves in Elixia. Atlas Ferraneir is the elf who is the current leader of the elves. He was your mother's close friend."

"Does Elixia have modern technology?" Lucy asked.

"It certainly could if you wanted, but past leaders have tended to keep Elixia the natural paradise that people normally think of."

"Makes sense," I said.

From the doorway Uncle Liam spoke up, "Who wants some dinner?"

Lucy

I gasped and sat up in bed, my mind whirling. Beads of sweat scorched my burning cheeks. I scrambled out of my sleeping bag and felt my way around in the darkness and crawled into the bathroom. I shut the door and leaned against it. I tried to erase my mind of the terrible nightmare. Was it a nightmare? I felt a small nagging in the back of my head that told me it wasn't. That told me it was real. That horrible night fifteen years ago. There was a woman in my dream. She had bright blonde hair with cool ice blue eyes. She was in a room of some sorts. It had marble floors and lace curtains. Two cradles rocked gently in the center of the room. Two sleeping princesses. I shook my head and willed my mind to shut off. I couldn't think about this anymore. I don't know why it was so frightening. Maybe it was because there was a man that had been standing beside the woman. A man that had looked frighteningly similar to my Uncle.

– – – * – – –

"Lucy?" A soft voice said. I opened my eyes and a familiar face filtered through my vision. I groaned and slowly sat up.

"Where am I?"

"Ummm, in the bathroom," Holly said as she supported my back. Everything came rushing back. I squeezed my eyes shut and took a deep breath.

"Are you okay?" Holly asked.

"I'm fine. What time is it?" I yawned.

"A little after four."

"Is anyone else awake yet?"

"No. I woke up to go to the bathroom and found you here on the ground."

"Oh,"

"Why are you in the bathroom?"

"I……. had a bad dream."

"Do you want to talk about it?"

"Not really."

"That's okay. Do you need anything?"

"No, I'm fine."

"Okay, well I need to go to the bathroom. Can you-"

"Oh, yes. Sorry."

"Thanks."

I decided to get up and look around the hotel before

everyone else woke up. I doubted that I would be able to fall back asleep. I slipped on my shoes and walked down the hall. I kept thinking about my dream. What did it mean? Was it what I thought it was? I needed answers. But I couldn't ask anyone. Could I? No. I would have to keep this to myself. Everyone else would think I was crazy. But deep down I knew that holding it in would just make it worse.

"Where are you going?" a voice said from behind me. I whirled.

"Why are you following me, Lucas?"

"I dunno."

"Did Calvin tell you to?"

"No, why would you think that?"

"Because I'm her guard and I'm supposed to keep her safe." Calvin stepped into view from behind a doorway looking very *very* tired.

"UGHHH! Can't I go *anywhere* without an escort?"

"Sorry. It's my job." Calvin said. I turned around and headed back toward the girl's room. So much for alone time.

"I'm going back to bed."

"That's fine with me." Calvin yawned. I rolled my eyes.

$- - - * - - -$

During breakfast, Holly kept looking at me expectantly. I had told her that I would tell her about my dream after breakfast. I guess my conscience had won. Or maybe it was my personality. I could NEVER hold anything in. I always had to tell someone. I didn't have any secrets that I kept to myself. The only way I could hold something in was if I promised someone

I wouldn't reveal their secrets. As we cleared our plates Holly came to stand beside me.

"Is now a good time?"

I glanced at Calvin, "Is there any way to get away from him?"

"I don't know. Probably not. Is it that bad if he knows?"

"I guess that's fine." I sighed and started walking toward the corner of the cafeteria. Just as I had expected, Calvin followed. I rolled my eyes.

"Wow. that eye roll was impressive," Holly said. I glared at her.

"Eye roll?" Calvin asked.

"Nothing," I said. "Calvin, go stand over there by the door." I pointed to a spot a few yards away where he could hopefully not hear us, but also be able to do his duty. I took a deep breath and began telling Holly about my dream.

"Oh my," was all Holly could say when I was finished.

"I don't know what to think," I said. Actually, I knew exactly what to think. I somehow just knew. I knew I had to stay away from Uncle Liam.

"Dang. I'm glad I don't get scary dreams," Calvin said.

"Ugh. I guess that wasn't far enough away. Why can't you give us some privacy?! And it wasn't scary. It was just. . . unsettling," I said.

"Whatever."

"Lucy!" Holly whispered harshly, "Maybe our powers are opposite! You can see the past and I can see the future! I wonder what the opposite of being a living lie detector is." I blinked.

"I-" I began.

"I hope we can go swimming today," Calvin said loudly. I was about to get after him for interrupting me when I noticed Lucas approaching followed closely by Victoria. I shot Calvin a grateful look. He smiled back.

"What are you guys talking about?" Victoria asked.

"How much we want to go swimming," Holly said. Lucas raised an eyebrow.

"I don't believe you," he said.

"Oh well," I said.

"Anyway, my mom needs you. She got a call from the Atlas guy," Victoria said. Holly and I shared a look.

"Let's go," I said.

We found Aunt Jane in our hotel room, making the beds.

"Hey," I said. Calvin waited just outside the door as Holly and I entered the room.

"Oh, hi girls." she said, "governor Ferraneir called. He said that we are welcome to go to Elixia right now but he will have to confirm that you are really the heir to the throne," She directed the last part at me. I wondered if Holly was ever sad or felt jealous about not inheriting the crown.

"When are we leaving?" Holly said.

"As soon as possible. Probably right after lunch."

"Where exactly is it?" I asked.

"It's on an island."

"Oh, cool." I said.

"It is pretty amazing. Before you step onto the island, it looks like a small mound of rocks. But, the moment you touch it, it expands into a huge thriving woodland."

"It's not a tropical place?" Holly said.

"No. That's one of the cool things about it."

"That's kinda weird," I said. Aunt Jane laughed.

"Can't wait to see it," I said.

My aunt smiled. "It's been so long since I've been there." There was a hint of sadness in her voice as she spoke. "I wonder if anything has changed." I didn't know what to say to that.

After a moment Holly broke the silence. "Do you need any help cleaning up?"

"Nope. But why don't you tell the others our plan?"

"Sounds good." I followed Holly out of the room.

Chapter Six

Holly

"Holly, Lucy? Can I talk to you for a sec?" Uncle Liam said as Victoria cleared the UNO cards off the table. We had decided to play a speed round of UNO before we left.

"Ummmm," I glanced at Lucy. She looked equally cautious.

"Okay,"sShe said. As we got up and followed Uncle Liam to the door, I saw Lucy look back several times to make sure Calvin was following us. Thankfully, he was. Uncle Liam led us outside and around to the back of the hotel.

"Ummm, Uncle Liam?" Lucy asked.

"Yes?"

"Where are we going?"

"I just need your help with something."

I guess Calvin was getting cautious as well because he stayed a lot closer to me and Lucy than he ever had before. Uncle Liam approached a black, fifteen passenger van. I stopped as my mouth dropped and my heart seemed to stop beating. Sitting on the hood of the car was a woman with bright blonde hair and blue eyes.

"Hello, Holly," Miranda slid off the car and approached us. Calvin stepped in front of us. For once, I could tell Lucy was grateful to have a bodyguard. "Now, now. Don't worry boy. I won't hurt your precious princesses," She turned back to me and Lucy and fingered my now blonde hair. "My, my. I can hardly tell the difference between you. Except, when you live with someone for fifteen years, it's hard to get them mixed up with a different person. Holly has always walked with a slight limp from the time her horse, Raven, stomped on her foot and shattered the bones."

"Get away from her," Calvin said.

"Excuse me, young man. Is that how you talk to your elders?"

"I'm sorry if I sound disrespectful, but my job is to protect them." My heart flipped when he said, 'protect *them*' instead of 'protect *Lucy*'.

"You think I'm going to prevent you from doing your job? Actually, don't answer that. I am." She signaled with her hand and immediately three big men came out from behind the dumpsters and surrounded us. Uncle Liam stepped forward and stood beside Miranda. I looked at Lucy and saw tears glistening in her eyes. Suddenly it hit me. Lucy had known Uncle Liam all her life. He had been like her father. I knew she and Uncle Liam had been very close. As close as they could get. I could practically see her heart breaking.

"Why?" she said. She spoke so quietly I was surprised I could hear her. I thought I saw a flash of regret in his eyes. But, if I did, it was only for a moment.

"Lucy. I do love you. You're like a daughter to me. I truly do want what's best for you. I just......" His voice cracked.

"Enough," Miranda said. She nodded to the three men. They stepped forward and attempted to grab our hands and tie them behind our backs. But before they were able to succeed, Calvin jerked out of one of the burly guy's grip and back knuckled him in the face, causing him to stumble backwards in shock. Blood trickled from his nose. I stared in surprise as he quickly grabbed a knife and gun out of the guy's belt. Then he pounced on Miranda slamming her to the ground. He pressed the point of the knife against her neck. I gasped. Miranda's eyes were wide with fright.

"Nobody move," he said. One of the men stepped toward him. Calvin aimed the gun at him and cocked it, causing the man to stop.

"Now. Move away from the girls." When they made no move to obey, Calvin pressed the blade harder against Miranda's neck. "Move away or she dies." Slowly they moved away but not before the guy behind me twisted my arm in a very wrong position to try to finish tying my hands together. I cried out in pain as I heard a snap. I think he was surprised that he had caused damage because he hurried the others a few feet away.

"Holly!" Lucy ran to my side and helped me up as I crumpled to the ground. The pain was so excruciating I felt like I was going to pass out. Lucy helped me over to sit behind Calvin. Sitting down definitely reduced the nausea. I noticed that only one other man carried a gun, which he now pointed at Calvin whose face was red with rage.

"You're going to regret that," Calvin said through his clenched teeth. He pressed the knife point into Miranda's neck even harder causing a trickle of blood to leak out and slide down her neck. She gasped.

"Stop!" One of the men said. Calvin grinned. He had struck a chord. He reduced the pressure on Miranda's neck.

"Tell them to get in the van," he said to her. When she did not reply, Calvin looked at her face. She had fainted. Probably as a result of shock. As I studied the men more closely I realized they all looked extremely alike. They were all bald and at least six and a half feet tall. They had huge bulging muscles that rippled at every move. The only differences were their faces.

"Trust me, you do not want to shoot that," Calvin said. The guy lowered the gun. But only slightly. "Go get in the van."

"Why should we obey you?" The guy who had been attacked by Calvin said as he held a handkerchief to his gushing nose.

"If you don't, she dies," Calvin motioned to Miranda. I

winced as I saw her shirt that now had a huge red splotch on the back. I looked away. She might have lied to me and been my enemy, but she was still the only person I had had for a mother.

He didn't give them a chance to answer, "What is your job? Why are you doing this?"

"Well, to make sure you won't get in the way of her taking over the elven world."

"Harrison!" One of the other guys said, "We weren't supposed to say that!"

The man called 'Harrison' blanched, "I-I forgot." As the men began accusing Harrison, A figure by the hotel caught my eye. Or rather two figures. I wanted to cry out loud with joy. It was Victoria and Lucas. If there was one thing I had learned over the past few weeks, it was that I should *never* get in a fight with Lucy, Victoria or Lucas. They were all VERY experienced in Karate and could take me out easily. They might not be able to defeat the men but they could at least do some damage. Surprise would be their best ally. I had wondered why Lucy hadn't gone all 'kung fu panda' on them, but I realized she was probably waiting for the right opportunity. I nudged Lucy's foot.

"What?" She asked.

"Look!" I whispered back. Her face broke out in a huge grin when she spotted our cousins. Victoria and Lucas were almost to the men. Victoria seemed to be talking on the phone with someone. Hopefully the police. Calvin had now seen them as well. Uncle Liam just stood on the side and seemed to be thinking about his life choices. *Good.* I thought. *Hopefully he regrets everything he ever did.* Another surge of pain and I found tears landing on my twisted arm.

"Hey!" Harrison shouted and whirled around. Lucas had snatched the gun out of his hand and before the other men had a chance to react, Lucas was already standing beside me. Victoria had also joined us.

"Who were you calling?" Lucy asked her.

"The police. They should be here any minute. "Just as she said that I heard sirens screaming in the distance, "What happened to your arm?" She looked at me, concern painted her face.

"One of the creepy weirdos bent my arm funny when he was trying to tie my arms together."

"Oh my goodness. It's swelling a lot."

"I think it's broken."

"Your face is as white as a sheet."

"It hurts a lot."

"I'm so sorry. You have a high pain tolerance." I nodded and we turned back to the others. The way we were positioned, they were cornered between us and the brick wall behind the hotel building.

"I suggest not fighting back. The police are almost here."

"Why should we be scared of children?" A man growled.

"Three of us are very experienced in karate, kung fu and jiu-jitsu, I have been training for fights like this for years and I know how to win in a fight."

"I bet we could beat you up in ten seconds," the same guy said.

"Not before we take care of you first." I turned my head as Aunt Jane approached with several security guards from the hotel. My heart leaped. Maybe we would win after all. I had to admit, at first, I wasn't sure we would survive this fight. Moments later three police cars pulled up. I stood up which was a bad idea because immediately a wave of dizziness crashed through my head. This time, I let it take me. I knew everything would work out. Everything faded away as I fell back into Victoria's arms.

Lucy

I watched anxiously as Holly slowly opened her eyes. She blinked several times and looked at me. I smiled back.

"How do you feel?" I asked.

"My arm hurts." She said, looking at her arm which was wrapped in a tan bandage.

"I am so sorry they did that," Calvin said from the doorway. Holly jerked up, clearly not expecting Calvin to be there too. Her face heated up. I grinned. She had never told me about her crush on Calvin but she made it quite clear. She was always very shy around him and whenever he looked at her, she looked like a tomato.

"It's not your fault. So, what happened last night after I fainted?"

"Well, the police just arrested all of them. They looked at the hotel's security cameras and found the proof they needed. So, everything's okay now." Holly looked away and stared out the window.

"It must be hard for you." Calvin said, coming to sit on the bed next to her.

"It is." Holly barely managed to choke out the words, "She was my mother. She acted like my mother at least. She would read to me when I was little. But it was all just a charade."

"I am so sorry you had to live like that," I said, "We have a surprise for you." Holly looked at me and searched my face. At that moment, a little girl with chocolate curls ran in, but as soon as she saw us she stopped. Holly stared and tears welled up in her eyes.

"Where's Holly?" Claire looked uncertain at us. Apparently she didn't recognize her with our dyed hair and blue eye contacts.

"Claire!" Holly slid off the bed and ran to embrace her sister. Claire looked startled for a minute then understanding sunk in. She wrapped her arms around Holly and buried her head in her neck. I couldn't imagine how she felt right now.

After a moment, Holly pulled back and asked, "How did you get here?"

"Aunt Jane came and picked me up. The police made mom tell where we lived."

"So she's actually your mom?"

"Yes. Sadly. Aunt Jane said I could live with you guys."

"I am so glad," Holly hugged her again.

"Why is your hair different?" Claire asked.

Holly smiled, "It's so no one can recognize us."

"Why would you want no one to recognize you?" Holly and I explained everything to her from the day at wal-mart to last night. When we were finished, we walked into the hotel lobby where everyone else was waiting.

"How do you feel?" Aunt Jane asked.

"Great. Thank you." Holly said, "How are *you*?" Holly searched her tear-stained face. As they continued their conversation, I walked over to sit beside Victoria and Lucas who were both sitting quietly in the corner and staring out the window.

"How's it going?"

"Fine," Lucas said.

"Do you need anything?"

"No," Victoria said.

"Okay." I returned to Aunt Jane, Holly, Calvin, and Claire. Aunt Jane was crying. We just sat with her. Holly was holding her hand. I squeezed my eyes shut to try to hold back the tears but somehow they managed to slip out. It was like a dam that had one tiny crack in it. Soon the 'water' was flowing freely and it was beyond my strength to stop it. About ten minutes later, when we had no more tears, Aunt Jane announced that she had two more surprises for Holly. Victoria and Lucas joined us as we walked outside to the parking lot. We approached a horse trailer. At first Holly looked confused but then her face lit up.

"Is it?" she couldn't finish her sentence.

"Yes!" Claire said, "We brought Raven!" Holly turned to Aunt Jane,

"May I?" She asked.

"Of course." Holly ran to the trailer and opened the back. A loud whinny greeted her. Seconds later she emerged with the most beautiful horse I had ever seen. Holly held a lead rope in her hand that she used to guide the horse.

"Thank you so much!" she said to Aunt Jane who smiled.

"You may have noticed that Raven is invincible?" She said,

"Yes, I did."

"Do you remember when your grandpa came to visit you?"

"Yes."

"He gave you this horse. She is actually a pegasus."

"Why doesn't she have wings?"

"This particular breed doesn't have wings but they can still fly."

"She can fly?????"

Aunt Jane laughed, "Yes, she can."

"You said you had *two* surprises, mom," Victoria said.

"Oh yes," Aunt Jane said. She whistled and a man got out of the truck that was pulling the trailer. Holly gaped. The man had dirty-blonde hair and green eyes. He was quite good looking and appeared to be in his late thirties.

"Dad?" Holly finally said.

"Hello, Holly,"

"How?...When?...." Holly asked.

"As it turns out, Aunt Jane is a Healer. The oldest sister or brother of the queen or king is a healer which means they can heal anyone from any sickness, disease or curse." The guy said.

"So she healed you?" Holly asked.

"She did."

"Wait, are you my *real* dad?" Holly barely breathed.

He smiled, "I am. Miranda cursed me when you guys were

little. She didn't want me to find you." My mouth fell open. This was my *dad*??? I thought he was dead! He turned to me and grinned.

"Lucy."

"I never thought I would see my father," I said, smiling.

"Well, here I am," He turned back to Holly, "You look very different with your hair dyed."

"I guess we can dye it back now." Holly said.

"I just started getting used to it," I said.

"You don't have to, I guess, but I am dying it back."

"I was kidding. I'm dying it back. Or I'll let it grow out. Actually, that would look kinda weird." Aunt Jane somehow managed to laugh.

"Then," she said as she pulled us all into a group hug, "Let's get you to Elixia."

The End

Jamie Allred

In Darkness Shall You Find Your Soul

Christopher JH Jones

Once upon a time, they tell me, is how you begin a story. Let it be so, then, although the words mean nothing to me. They don't mean anything at all, when you come to it. But we use them just the same, and all pretend they make sense.

Thinking about it, that's a pretty good metaphor for my life at the moment.

I'm sitting on the tailgate of a rusting 1970s-era pickup truck, my tattered jeans taking on more and more of the color of oxidized metal and flaking green paint, while I try to decide whether I should let the jostling of the truck pitch me out the back onto the dirt road that seems to spool like fishing line away behind me, endlessly.

It rained that morning, and even though the high mountain air dries out the soil faster than the clouds can put it down, seems like, the road's dust is staying put and not coating me as it usually does. I take that as a blessing. There have been few enough of them, recently.

Behind me in the bed of the truck are three more young men, in their late teens like me, dirty like me, in faded jeans like me. They work at the failing silver mine like me. But they are not like me. They know it, and I know it.

Driving the truck is perhaps the meanest woman I've ever known, and my own mother was so mean she sold me for a case of T-bone steaks when I was twelve. She—the driver, not my mother—is named Esme Montgolfier, but is called Goldie to her face and other things when her back is turned. She has short-cropped hair and a face so weatherbeaten I wonder if she spent a decade as a scarecrow, hanging in a field, shouting random swear words in eccentric spasms of hopeless fury. Since she does this to the four of us, I figure she had to have practiced somewhere. Or maybe she was always like this.

Stretching away to the horizon is a sky so blue, so pale blue, that it is nearly white, without a cloud in it, though as I mentioned it rained this morning. We're climbing slowly up the side of a mountain. If *it* has a name, I don't know it. The sixteen of us that work the mine call it The Pit.

The truck hits a particularly nasty rut and bucks like a riled-up steer. My butt comes up off the tailgate six inches or more and I have to haul myself back down or go rolling down the mountainside. And what if I did? Might break something on the rocks, lie there and starve. But they'd miss me directly and come find me, and Goldie might chew off a finger. I'd never actually seen her do it, but she always looked like she might. And that was when she was in a good mood.

They would come look for me. There was no way they'd let me go. It's nice to be needed, is another one of those things people say, but I mostly think that gets said by folks that aren't.

I'm needed, all right. And right now that keeps me fed and warm...well, not too cold, anyway...and there are worse things than crawling around on your hands and knees in the frigid dark ten hours a day.

I think. Probably there are. There must be. Though that afternoon I couldn't think of any.

Sometimes life carries you forward along a channel that you didn't pick and don't really understand, but you and everyone else just float along with it even though it makes no sense. Maybe I could take action, get away, go somewhere, but with what money? Why, also, is the bigger question. This is a bad place with bad people, and I don't like it. But I'd never been anyplace I *did* like so you can forgive me if I wasn't right sure there was any point in making a break for it, if you know what I mean.

I scratch at an itchy place on my scalp and run my dirty hands through my shoulder-length hair. Can't grow a beard, but my hair grows like I'm an ad for Rogaine. The truck bucks. The three others stare at the rusting bed and breathe in and out, thinking unreadable thoughts. I stare back along the unspooling road. Soon enough we'll be at The Pit, and they'll stick us in the basket and lower us down, and I'll go crawling through the black, waiting for the stabbing fire in my chest that means I've touched the metal.

#

I don't know what the metal is. I've seen it, in its crumbled form, mixed with rock and dust and often blood–a light tan that looks vaguely like loose dirt where a dog took a dump in it. It's hard, though, when I touch it, not squishy, and it has to be hacked from the guts of the mountain with picks and swearing. Their picks. My swearing.

Once I've found it, I can't swing a pick anymore, not for hours. There's no warning. I crawl around in the dark, into tunnels that sometimes have headroom and sometimes not. I can't wear a headlamp, because...ah, hell, I better tell it all.

When I was twelve, my mother sold me to a traveling salesman for a case of T-bone steaks, which I said before, but maybe you didn't believe me. It's true. The salesman was short and slimy and massively overweight and the steaks were probably horse or dog or something but he charmed my mother like one of those Indian fakirs charms a cobra and before I knew it I was being shoved into the back of a puke-green station wagon with the rest of the frozen meat and driven down the street. The door didn't open from the inside and there was a cage that kept me from getting up to the driver and strangling him. As if the Pied Stake Salesman did this kind of thing a lot.

He drove me to a warehouse by the docks, right against the river, with me hollering and screaming at him–the cage stopped my body, but it didn't mute my voice any. The big door rolled up, gray as slate, and rolled back down behind us, cutting off any light but the little bulb that came on when he opened the door. He shut it, and the light disappeared, and he left.

I don't know how long I was in there–long enough to start worrying away at the lid of one of the boxes to get at the raw meat inside–but the guy did eventually come back, swinging a flashlight. And a bat. Which he hit me with the second he opened the back gate of the wagon. I screamed and rolled out and smacked onto a gritty concrete floor.

"Don't want you getting any ideas," he said, calm as a summer day, while I writhed on the floor holding my leg. I thought it was broken, but it wasn't. If it had been, this next part wouldn't have happened and I wouldn't spend every day in The Pit now. But maybe I'd have been locked back in the wagon and pushed into the river, too, so look on the bright side. Or the dark side, more like. You get the idea.

"Stroke of luck, my running into you," he said, like we was both out walking dogs or something. Old pals from college. "I was going to have to pick up some trash from the gutter, but now...you've got meat on your bones. Much better."

He grabbed my arm and twisted it up into the flashlight's beam. Despite his waddle and the truck tire of fat on the guy, he had muscle and I couldn't break his grip. He sniffed and ran a sausage-like finger over the smooth skin of the inside of my arm. "No needles. Lucky me."

There was a noise from down inside the bowels of the warehouse and two more flashlights came bobbing along. Two more guys, I thought, but it wasn't, just one guy and a woman that looked like a cross between an orc and a rabid wolverine.

"This the kid?" the new man said, in a voice like crunching gravel.

"No," my guy said, still calm and reasonable, "I got six more in the wagon. Yes, of course this is the kid."

The woman–I was still grunting in pain and twisting in the half-inch dust on the concrete floor, but she stuck her flashlight practically up my nose and peered at me with eyes as black as Satan's heart. "He looks like a runner."

My guy took the bat and whacked my other leg. On the ankle.

"Not anymore."

I screamed and cried and couldn't understand why God hated me so much.

The three of them went over a little way and started having a conversation about something, probably me, but I couldn't hear through my screaming and couldn't see through my tears, and they ignored me as if I was bolted down.

I wasn't, though. And I was hurt but I was twelve, and at twelve your body does miracles of recovery and long before I stopped screaming I stopped hurting so bad I needed to scream, so when I thought there was a chance I shucked up to my knees and went to bolt.

But it was dark. Reflection from the flashlights showed me only the butt end of the car and thick black beyond it, but no wall, and maybe there was a door over there, or I could hide, or...I was twelve, and critical thinking wasn't a thing yet. But anywhere away from Steak Man and the bat was better than this.

The floor was dusted, not thick, but just enough that my worn-out sneaks wouldn't grab. My feet spun like Roadrunner but just like him they eventually got grip and I shot across the concrete toward...well, whatever there was in the dark over there. Nothing, was what I was hoping. My ankle and shin howled like wolves but fear is a great painkiller. I probably would have made it.

But I crashed into some metal barrels with a noise like the trump of doom and we all went down in a heap. Something syrupy sheeted over me. It smelled like spoiled milk mixed with rotten eggs. There was a lot of it, and it coated my head, my neck, right down my shirt and into my pants. Cold, too. I spluttered and coughed and then some of it got in my mouth and if I thought it smelled bad the taste was like licking Lucifer's armpit.

Of course they were on me before I could even think of rolling over, which I couldn't do because I was about to vomit.

"Oh, for the love of...the kid's coated in Stuff," the new man said, while the steak salesman laughed like the wheezing of a rusted radiator and the woman just stood there, cold as sin, staring.

"Get up, kid," he said, but I couldn't have gotten up for the keys to a Ferrari. I lay there, covered in stinking goop, my ankle and my shin throbbing, surrounded by people who buy children with steaks, and–this is the really funny part–thought my life couldn't possibly get worse.

It only took three, maybe four more seconds for the universe to play the ace of spades.

Steak man finally finished laughing and got a rag from one of the barrels. He reached down and gripped my pant-leg and hauled. Slick as I was, everything in the pile around me shifted and one of the barrels, already tipped and unbalanced, fell over. Rocks and dirt rained down on me.

All at once, I forgot about the stench. I forgot about my ankle. I forgot about my shin. I forgot about having been sold into slavery.

Every nerve in my body lit up, shrieking like someone was running a rusty file over them. Like I'd been submerged in acid. Like a million tongues of flame licked my skin, my bones, inside, outside, every atom in me burned.

I must have been screaming, because my throat was raw for days afterward, but I couldn't hear it. Every muscle seized and my body went rigid, arched, fingers curled and arms locked, legs spasming. Nothing but pain. Like no pain that ever was or ever could be. Thought fled and there was only the agony, white-hot and zero-cold, on and on for days.

Could not have been days. Could not have been more than a few seconds. I would never have survived.

But I did survive. There were hands brushing me, cutting off my clothes, wiping goop off me, and I was lying naked on the concrete, shivering, cramping, making the whimpering noise a beaten dog makes.

"What the hell was that?" new man whispered.

In answer, the woman took a handful of goop and slopped it on my chest. I lay there, spent, inert, like a rag doll without stuffing. She took a rag and wiped it off.

Then she trickled a palmful of rocks onto me and the agony began again.

"...something to do with the rock."

"An allergy or something?"

"Worse than any allergy I ever saw."

"We can't test it any more. It'll kill the kid."

"If he ain't dead already."

"If he's dead I'll jump in the river myself. But if he's not, if he reacts like that to—"

"He's awake," the woman said.

They came to stand over me, like scientists dissecting a cadaver.

"You hear me, kid?" Steak Man said.

I might have wanted to nod, somewhere in the back of my brain, but even if I had, I couldn't. My body refused instructions.

"Blink if you can hear me."

Why should I give him anything? I thought. But I blinked.

The man exhaled, a great gust of relief. He shook his head and chuckled. He was a great one for humor, this guy. "You had me worried. For a minute there I thought the most valuable kid in the world was a goner."

The what?

"Good work finding him," new man said.

"He didn't mean to find him," the woman said. "He gets no thanks."

"I don't want thanks," Steak Man said. "I want a very large amount of money."

New man spluttered. "That's not...we don't..."

The woman swore. Colorfully. At length. Finally she wound down and said, "Get the man his money."

New man gaped like he was watching the ascension of Jesus. "M-money? For him?"

She didn't say anything, just turned those inhuman eyes on him and he deflated like a pricked balloon. He scurried off, a rat in the darkness.

"Well, I must say I wasn't expecting you to be so reasonable," Steak Man said, turning toward his vehicle.

If I had been capable of speech, I would have maybe tried to cry out or something, warn him, because as much as this dude had bought me right off my front porch and then whacked me with a bat, the woman was a different kind of evil. And I knew the moment his back was turned she would strike.

Her arm whipped out and at the end of it something glittered and rattled like the tail end of a snake. It wrapped around Steak Man's neck once, twice, and caught. He reared back like a bucking horse but she was a rider, her boots planted on his hips and the cords of muscle in her arms standing out like taut rope. He thrashed, and he was strong, but she was a viper and her fangs were deep in his flesh. He tottered against the side of the car. He slumped to his knees, grappling for the chain around his neck.

He toppled onto the concrete. He lay still.

She clung anyway, her face a mask, not letting go.

Finally she trusted that he was dead, and clambered off him. She took him under the arms and dragged him to the back of the wagon. I wouldn't have believed a woman that slight could hoist a man that big, but she did it, though it took her a couple of minutes and she had to rest once, the only time I've ever seen her show human weakness.

But she got it done in the end. She slammed the wagon's rear gate and climbed into the front seat and put the old rustbucket in neutral. Then she climbed back out again and went to the front of the car. She pushed a button on a thick wooden post and the garage door rolled up about five feet. She put her hands flat on the hood of the car, and pushed.

The car rolled back with a gentle crunch. It picked up a little speed going down the lip of the garage ramp, and rolled serenely across the narrow road. There was a little metal lip, like a curb, on the border of the asphalt where it met the river's edge, and the car whumped up when it struck, but it had just enough momentum to get over, and then it was ground to a halt, teetering, metal on metal, until the woman walked out of the garage, across the road, and put the heel of her boot on the front fender.

Her leg cocked and straightened, and with a squeal the car slid backward and vanished. There was a splash, but not as big as I would have expected. She dusted off her hands, walked back into the garage, and rolled the door down.

A flashlight bobbed in the distance and the new man–the only man, now–arrived, out of breath, with a bulging sack. "I didn't know how much…"

He looked about, bewildered, eyes roving over the spot where the car had been as if it were hiding in the middle of the floor. "Lance?" he finally said.

"Had to go."

"Will he be back?"

The woman didn't reply. Her boots thudded over to me, and she looked down.

Those eyes said, "I know you saw that. And if you ever say a word, you'll end up with him."

Then the boots thumped away, and the flashlight left with them.

#

I came to still on my back but not on the concrete anymore. Fabric and metal underneath me. My breathing, something about the sound, told me before I opened my eyes that I was in a room, and it was small. I groaned. Every muscle protested any attempt to move.

But I opened my eyes at last and saw my new home. About ten feet by six, cinderblock walls, high ceiling–probably fifteen feet or so–from which dangled a single bare incandescent. It was off.

IN DARKNESS

I lay on a cot, one of those old army jobs, canvas and pipe. Slowly, like a hundred-year-old man, I swung my legs off the cot and down to the concrete floor. A door was set in the wall behind me, a great metal thing with a window of reinforced glass about the size of both my palms together. It let in enough light for me to see. In one corner was what I assumed was meant to be a john–it sort of looked like a potty-trainer–and above it to the right a metal sink jutted from the wall.

That was it. Well, almost. On the wall opposite the door was one of the largest flat-screen TVs I ever saw. And the remote perched like a bird on the top lip of it.

I wanted to stand, and go over to it, but my legs wouldn't support me. I wobbled and fell back on the cot and lay there, gasping like I'd run a sprint.

There was a twisting groan and someone opened the door. They switched on the light. I had to shut my eyes against the blinding of it and still it burned. But that went away and I saw who had come to visit me.

It was not who I expected.

It was a girl.

No, not the woman with eyes like the fathomless pit, but a girl. Might be about my age. Tall, willowy, coltish with legs and arms her body hadn't caught up with. She had a long face and freckles framed by hair that might have been a sort of reddish-brown if it were washed. She wore overalls over a shirt so dirty it might have been one of the rags from the garage.

She walked over to me and her feet made no sound on the floor. No shoes.

"Hi," she said. Like we met in the halls at school and I was the new kid.

"--" I said, because some bits of me weren't working just yet. My mouth worked. It opened and closed. My lungs worked, because duh. But when I tried to hook them together to make sounds, something didn't connect.

She nodded as if that meant something, my gasping like a landed fish, and held up a glass of water. The glass wasn't clean. The water wasn't, either, dull rust-brown color you could barely see through. She just held it there, waiting.

I tried to lift a hand, found I could, and took hold of the glass.

"Careful now. Don't drop it," she said.

My hand shook and a little water spilled out and spattered on the cot, but I got the glass to my mouth eventually and sipped. It burned going down.

"Try it now," she said.

"Gchfuh," I said.

She very nearly smiled. But not quite.

"Thank...you," I managed. Raspy, nothing like my real voice, but intelligible.

"You're welcome. I thought you'd be thirsty."

My eyes roved around the room, such as it was, and rested back on her. "How long?"

"Have you been here? A little over a day, at this point. I checked on you. You were sleeping."

I felt like it. I also felt like I could sleep some more. A lot more.

My stomach lurched and rumbled, but didn't toss the water back up. After a moment, I risked a bit more. The water wasn't any better, but my stomach stayed put.

"I'm Katulka," she said, touching her chest as if I might not understand otherwise.

She waited patiently for my name–in time I came to recognize that she did everything that way, with a calm and a patience like a Franciscan nun—but I didn't feel like supplying it. I drained the water and grimaced at the metallic taste and laid my head back on the cot and closed my eyes. I might not have gone instantly back to sleep, but I have no memory of Katulka taking the glass from my hand.

#

It took two days for me to be able to stand up, and another day before I could walk without help. I never saw anyone but Katulka, but she came regularly—I guess it was regular—and brought me food and water and something infinitely more precious, something I don't remember ever getting from anyone else.

The second day she told me about the TV. I couldn't walk yet so she plucked the remote from its perch above the set and handed it to me. She sat down on the floor by the cot. I swiveled to be able to see the screen, my bare feet dangling over the side of the bed, and pressed the red button at the top of the black handheld.

The TV flared to life, bright in that dim space. It asked me what I wanted to watch and gave me a menu of choices. A large menu.

"What are these things?" I said.

"A TV and a remote?" she asked, clearly skeptical that I could be that out of touch.

I scowled. I didn't want her to think I was dumb. "The boxes on the screen. Are those things to watch?"

"They're channels. Didn't you have cable, um, before?" At this point I knew nothing about her and I wasn't volunteering anything about myself.

"No." I didn't want to say we had a TV but it broke when one of my mother's boyfriends threw a bowling ball at it. And through it. After that it didn't work so well, but it hadn't really worked before, because all my mother ever watched was reruns of Gunsmoke.

"Point the remote at the TV and pick one of the boxes."

I had to scan the remote for a second to find a series of buttons in a loose circle that probably meant up and down. I pushed some of them and an arrow appeared, pointing to a thing called "Netflix", which I had heard of from the kids in the neighborhood. I pushed another button, the one in the middle, and the screen changed to a moving logo and a sound like an electric guitar slammed into the tiny room.

Katulka put her hands over her ears–too late–and I found buttons that said "Vol", plus and minus, and turned the 100 down to 20.

Netflix had a lot of stuff on it.

So did Amazon Prime. And Paramount. And TED. And...well, there were a lot of channels. I had a lot of time. We became friends.

By the count on the TV–it knew what date and time it was– I was in the room a month before anyone else came to see me. Not all the time, now, I did get to go out for walks around the warehouse, and pretty soon most of my strength came back and I could surely have overpowered Katulka and left. But...to where? "Home"? Wouldn't *that* dig up some unpleasant questions. I had nowhere to go.

And in that room, in that compound, I was getting food, more food than I was used to, and a little exercise, and nobody hassled me and I watched TV and talked to Katulka. Not in equal amounts, probably 2 to 1 for the TV. But I talked to Katulka more than any other human in the history of my life.

She was interesting. She was...interesting.

I also got acquainted with the compound. Every door was chained shut, so going outside wasn't an option, but there was plenty of interior space, most of it empty, bordered with rusty barrels full of electronic components, wire, LEDs, batteries, car parts, all sorts of stuff. I tinkered, but I had never been good at things like that.

When Katulka was gone to school–she walked down the road about a mile, and walked back–I watched TV, and it wasn't long before I got bored with the shows and started watching the History Channel and HGTV and TED and a ton of others. YouTube was a revelation. Lotta junk there–I got caught in some of it for a while–but I could learn anything I wanted if I was a little selective. So I was. And I did.

And in a month or so Goldie came to see me. I woke up and she was standing there. Might have been there for an hour, all I know. I scrambled back against the wall and huddled there as if it would stop her from eating me. Or whatever she was going to do.

When I found out, I wished she'd eaten me after all.

"You can find things for me," she said.

"I...what?"

She held out the dog poop metal, flat in her hand, a turd of hard rock. If I could have scrambled back through the wall, I would have.

She came a pace closer.

"Ah!" I cried out and slammed back against the wall.

"This," she said, "you can find. You'll find it for me."

She put the rock behind her and I slumped down on the cot.

"It hurts." I don't know why I said that, because she knew it and that was the point, anyway.

"Good thing, too," she said. Her had whipped out and grabbed my ankle. She threw me off the cot and I banged against the door.

She stood over me, tapping a boot on the concrete. "Still too weak. Another month."

"Mhmm," said Katulka, who was apparently just outside the door.

They fed me another month, and I learned about geology and volcanic action and pyroclastic flows and hypoglycemic shock. And Ted Lasso. Stupid show. As if there really are people in the world that are that nice.

Katulka watched with me, sometimes. One day I asked her if Goldie was her mother. She just stared at me, ice-blue eyes clear and wide and totally inscrutable. I took that as a "no", but I had no confidence in it.

A month later they took me to the mine.

The black pit of Hell could not have been less inviting, but they shoved me in and put three bigger boys behind me to plug up the escape.

"Find the stuff," Goldie said.

"Sulfur," I said. By now I'd had time with geology and I knew what I was looking at.

She hit me in the chest and the breath went out of me like a punctured balloon.

"Do not try to be smart," she said, and shoved me into the hole.

I said I wouldn't do it, so Goldie fired up a blowtorch and aimed it at my leg. I discovered I was wrong. I would do it.

She gave one of the boys the blowtorch. I found that out the hard way.

Anyhow, I had a light strapped to my head, a small bulb that didn't light up much of anything but was far, far better than the alternative. I crawled. For a long time. Late that first day I heard a whistle ricocheting like a bullet down the empty shafts and one of the boys behind me grabbed my ankle. I kicked out at him but he was stronger than I was and he dragged me back. After a minute I realized he was dragging me out of the tunnels.

By the fifth day, when we hadn't found anything, the mood was sour and there was some arguing between the boys and Goldie, which ended with one of the boys on the ground cradling his arm and the rest of us hustling into the mine. But that was a very bad day.

Sometime after the noon break for water one of the boys behind me yelled out, "Hé, *gazficko*, what's this? You no find this?"

I turned back as best I could–the tunnel today was wider than normal, and there was room overhead, enough that I could crouch–and there he was, holding a chunk of mustard-colored rock. It was the same stuff that locked me up before–or it sure looked like it–and he threw it at me. It scored my cheek as it flew by, rolling down the tunnel, skittering like a bat in the dark.

I braced myself. Nothing happened. No seizure. No rictus of pain.

I actually laughed. I know what it sounds like, but I did.

The boy yelled up to someone, and they yelled back, and he grabbed my ankle and hauled and we went back up. I was happy. My specialness was gone, and now they would let me stop scrabbling in the dark for the cursed stuff.

Goldie hit me on the side of the head with a chunk of the metal. Stars erupted around the bright hole of my vision and I catapulted sideways to land in a heap by the wheel of a tractor. Everything swam. My light had been thrown off to land a couple yards away. I felt a trickle of something warm down the side of my face.

"Useless," Goldie said. "Dump him."

She threw the rock at me, and when it thudded into my chest I exploded in agony.

#

Two days later, or so Katulka said, I came to in my cell and she explained something about the electromagnetic interference of the lamp with my sensitivity. So from that time on I didn't get a lamp.

I revived and got stronger and time went on and I learned a lot and suffered a lot and grew a little. Every time I would find some of the stuff they'd drag me out of the hole and dump me in the back of the truck and after a little while Katulka would come and start it up and drive me to the compound. She'd drag me up to my room and bring me water, and sit with me while I sipped.

As for Katulka, she grew up a little, too, and I started really wanting to find the metal in the dark, because when I did, even though the torture of the finding was a crucifixion it meant a couple of months where I saw Katulka every day.

She rounded, and firmed, and washed. Clean, she was a breath of heaven, talking to me about her day, what happened in school, how the flowers looked, just...anything. I listened for any mention, however slight, of boys, but she said nothing about them. I watched for any indication that she was feeling the same thing for me that I was for her, but again, nothing. She remained an unaccountable, impossible bloom in a barren wasteland of horror.

I tried a hundred times to ask her why she was there, why she was helping these psychopaths, but she never answered questions like that. Psychology videos led me to the idea that people's prisons are mostly in their minds. I began to wonder which of us was really the prisoner here.

One time I happened to fall through a weak patch in the floor. I thudded into the ground and began screaming like never before, or so they told me. I had no memory of it. Apparently it was an entire cavern of the stuff, and if they hadn't fished me out within a couple of minutes I would surely have just petrified right there in the cave. I broke a bone in my leg and three ribs–not from the fall, but from the muscular spasms that racked my body like a torturer's wheel. I bit through my tongue. The skin on the right side of my face was torn from grinding it on the cave floor.

This time, it took almost three months for me to recover and the ordeal was bad enough I started thinking of escape.

Well, I mean, I'd thought of escape before. And you, reading this, you've been wondering all along why I didn't escape long before this. Well, a couple reasons. One, I didn't really know–not for sure–that there were better places. For every Ted Lasso there was a Jigsaw. It was just TV, after all. I had lived in the world and where I was wasn't terribly much worse than that.

Two, the compound was locked up all day. Possibly there was a way through the chains and padlocks, if you really wanted there to be, but the incentive was not very strong, because three, they would catch me. Walking around the derelict neighborhood, no money, nothing, I was going to stand out and either Goldie would get me or someone else would.

One of the other fellas had made a break for it one morning, right at the mouth of the Pit, screaming about how he couldn't go down into the dark another day. Bolted into the brush and disappeared.

They brought him back before the shift ended and pushed him down a tunnel. He cried out, and there was a sound like a waterfall and a scream and then they put us all in the truck and drove us back to the compound.

The next morning he was still screaming. By now his voice was ragged and hoarse, but we could hear him, his crying echoing in the fathomless dark.

Four days. By then his voice was just a whisper.

Some days I can still hear it, crawling in the bowels of the earth. But all of us knew if we tried it, something just like that would happen to us.

So we searched, and when we found, the bigger boys dug and hauled and filled wagons–I rarely got to see this part, because I was almost always on my back in my cot–and Goldie's money piled up.

Oh, yeah. The money.

The compound–warehouse, whatever–was three stories tall, an empty barn of a building, with one wall of rooms for various things like keeping young people prisoner. Semi-prisoner. Like a cell block, with cells only on one side and the rest open space. Anyway on the ground floor, in rooms barred and barren, Goldie lived. We didn't go in, just looked through the reinforced windows set into thick metal doors painted a dusty industrial gray.

My cell was cheerless and sparse. So was hers.

"The money goes in, but it never comes out," Katulka said. She whispered, as if afraid to wake the ghosts.

"Money?"

She nodded. "Bags of it. Cash. She goes off to...somewhere...the bank, I guess, and she comes back with bags of money. Then she carries them in here and the door swings shut. And that's it."

"She must spend some," I whispered.

She made a face at me like I was too simple to have a conversation with. "On *what*?"

And I could think of nothing. Not furniture, for certain. Her truck was a thousand years old, like everything else. The tools the boys used at the mine were as scarred and beaten as she was.

"Internet access," I finally said, and we had to cover our faces to hide the snorts of laughter.

It was, though, incomprehensible. There were other people at the mine, but they were all underlings. It was Goldie in charge, everywhere, all the time. What was she getting from all this? Money was stupid unless you did something with it, like having a car that just sat in the garage or a magic rock-finder that didn't find rocks.

I found them. But it was excruciating. And it got worse.

After the three-day horror of the submersion in the stuff, I only found one more deposit–a small one, it seemed like, from the sour reaction of the boys–but it laid me up totally unconscious for two days and sipping broth from Katulka's spoon for the better part of a week.

Goldie came for a visit on day five or six and threw the cot– with me on it–across the floor. I didn't get up. I couldn't have. I just laid there in the dust with my nose bleeding and the cot's rail digging into my midsection. For good measure, she laid a vicious kick into my leg, thudding like a sack of rice. When I didn't move, she grunted.

"Thought he was faking," she said, apparently to Katulka, as she clomped out.

I wondered about that for a long time. Goldie never had an opinion. Never said anything she didn't have to. For her, that was a whole Shakespearean soliloquy (thanks, YouTube). The rocks of the mine were chatterboxes next to her. But she said she thought I was faking, loud enough for me to hear. More, she said it to Katulka.

Goldie left and a little after her boots had clanged down the metal staircase toward the floors below I felt Katulka's cool hand brush the back of my neck. She moved the cot, her arm slid around my waist and tugged and *now* I had something in me to get up, where I hadn't before. My leg throbbed and there was blood on my face, but her lips were next to my ear and she said, so low I might have imagined it, "you might have been faking."

She fixed me on the cot and brought water and broth and I got better, though an ache stayed in my knees and hips that never quite left, this time. For a month I staggered like a drunk or a seventy-year-old, but eventually some of the bounce came back. I took to jogging around the compound's interior, trying to get up some strength, because this time–this time–I knew I would want it.

Katulka never said another thing about faking it. She said plenty of other things, about books she was reading and her teachers at school. But then, other things she never talked about before, like places she wanted to go, and things she dreamed of seeing.

"Saw that," I said once about the Taj Mahal as she dreamily pronounced herself in love with it.

"On YouTube?" she said, a little sadly. "Don't you know that there are some things you can't learn from watching a screen?"

I looked at her face then, the far-off vision in her eyes, the freckles, the creamy skin like bleached silk, and the way a single lock of hair curled under her chin and thought, yes, I do know that.

But there were other things you *could* learn, and I worked hard to learn them.

Eventually, of course, they sent me back into the mine, and there I am, on the back of the truck, headed for the day's habitual torture, perhaps this day spiced with some actual torture, too.

Though I think not. Because...well. Because.

The truck jounces and bucks and then the road levels off onto gravel and it's just vibration all the way to the mouth of the Pit. My hands buzz where they'd gripped the tailgate, fizzing like they were electrified.

We climb down from the truck bed and stand around for a minute while chains are unlocked and doors grated aside, and then they shove us into the dark where a lift carries us down to the lower workings, a bit we'd been in for a couple of weeks, hunting. I hadn't found anything.

You couldn't always see it, the stuff, because sometimes it was mixed with other rock and sometimes it was in a crack deeper than the surface inch, but I could always feel it, if I got close enough.

At the bottom of the shaft I get out with the other three—guys I'd worked with a bunch, Jorge and Sasha and Amreet, not bad guys, just doing what they were told. Maybe they'd been bought for cuts of meat, too, although by now I am pretty sure that isn't a regular thing.

Anyway we pile out and I stand there like I didn't know which way to go until Sasha grabs my shoulder and frog-marches me down a sloping tunnel, his light bouncing off the slickdamp walls until we can't walk and then we crouch and then crawl, and hi ho, hi ho.

I get out ahead of them ten yards or so, my usual place. Grit under my elbows and hundreds of feet of rock over my head. Home, as much as anyplace is.

This tunnel is mostly natural, as I'd come to understand most of the honeycomb Pit was. Some of it has been hacked, but a lot of it is simple void in the volcanic rock. I used to imagine it was carved out by ants the size of large dogs, like Ender's Formics, tunnels never quite enough to stand up in, until the stooping and waddling overcame your thigh muscles and you were forced to crawl.

I have also long since observed that I had more freedom of movement than my minders did, as I was smaller and thinner, so I could move more easily through the ant-tunnels. It isn't hard to put significant distance between me and them. I don't do it much, because what's the point? The tunnels are a labyrinth and they are Ariadne. My connection to them is my connection to getting back out.

In the silence of the caves they can easily hear me, even if they can't see me, and besides, where would I go?

But they *can't* see me, unless their light is trained on my feet, and they can't see anything else. They won't dare not have their lights on.

I, however, am forbidden to use one, lest it interfere with my Midas touch. I do everything by touch. And after a few years in the dark I am very, very good at touch.

Ten yards ahead of my watchers, I reach into my pocket and draw out a small, lozenge-shaped plastic device with a little switch on it. I flip the switch and a dull red light glows through the plastic. It would be invisible in the dim bulb of my room, let alone the blaze of daylight, but in that Stygian dark it glows like the dying sun of Charn. A low-wavelength light. It won't carry and there is no way the flashlight-blind followers can see it, even if I shine it at them.

Which I do not.

I don't know if today will be the day. I don't know if it will come tomorrow, or the next day, or the day after that. But since all the days are the same day, that doesn't matter. One day will be the day.

The glow lights up the portion of tunnel ahead. I see none of the yellow stuff—it would be a fire-engine red under this light—but I think I might see some soon. The smell, maybe, or perhaps just that it has been two weeks, which is nowhere near the longest I'd gone without a strike, but we are getting into where it is more likely than not.

The day, such as it is, crawls on. As do I.

We stop for "lunch", a few slices of hard salami and some tasteless cheese, washed down with a thermos of water, and then I go on. The tunnel forks. I go right, slightly downward again, and within five yards there is the prize I seek.

Gleaming red, a vein the width of my forearm and yards long stretches into the glowing carmine night.

I put the lozenge in my pocket, careful not to turn off the switch. Then I reach down my pants and switch on a headlamp.

Yes, my pants. If there is any place they'll avoid touching while hauling my apparently spasming carcass from the Pit, it is my crotch. The only place I know I can hide something from them.

Then I scream.

It is very difficult to mimic the scream of someone in true agony. It takes considerable practice to master it, but master it I had in the long hours alone in my cell. I was, if I do say so myself, completely convincing, though because of the hidden electronic device, I felt nothing.

I mimic all of it. The rictus, the spasm of muscles, the wide, white-rimmed eyes, I do it all and I do it well, and Jorge is first to get to me and finds the vein of stuff right away. Of course I'd be convulsing. He passes me back to Amreet and he slides me, periodically shrieking like a demon of Hell, back to Sasha, who together with Amreet carries me to the lift and takes me topside.

This is the hardest part.

It is so, so bright up there, even inside the mouth of the cave, that I simply can't trust myself not to blink. Instead, as they're taking me out of the lift I have a particularly violent spasm that breaks me loose from their grip and tumbles me down a pair of stone steps, where my scream abruptly cuts off and I lie on my face as inert as an unstuffed scarecrow.

"He's dead," Sasha says, a ribbon of fear in his voice.

I feel the vibration of boots on rock, and know she is coming. Fingers on my neck, rough like a gravel road. My heart hammers away–no chance she doesn't feel my pulse.

"Not dead," Goldie says.

I have to stay limp for what comes next. It will be worse if I don't.

As it is, the boot thudding into my leg nearly made me cry out. But I don't. I don't move. I keep my breathing shallow and my face planted in slategrit and I lie motionless.

Pause. Long. Too long?

"Truck," Goldie says.

They toss me in like a haybale and close the tailgate and leave.

I have to admit, I nearly fall asleep. You can only keep going on adrenaline for so long.

But there are so many things to hear, to feel. The powder of the dust in the truckbed. The way the rib of the corrugation of the pickup bed dug *here* and *here* and *here*. Birds in the trees. The sigh of wind. Low voices, discussing how rich the vein would be this time. The electronic squawk of a radio.

"They're on the way up."

"Feel bad for the kid."

"Don't. He knifed his mother and brother and dumped the guy who tried to rescue them into the river. I'd just as soon lock the mine and leave him in it."

Ah. Well, that explains some things.

The truck rocks gently and a door closes and the engine rumbles to life. We go down the mountain, down onto paved roads, and a little way through a quiet, crumbling part of a once-thriving town, and stop and wait a moment.

The thrum of an electric motor and the squeak and roll of a metal door on casters, gliding up.

We roll forward and into the dark space and the door rolled down. I hear the tailgate drop and feel the jounce of the springs as someone climbs into the truck.

Cool, smooth fingers on my neck. The breath of a whisper in my ear.

"You can get up now."

I roll over and above me is Goldie.

Her foot is already cocked back to strike at my ribs and I know what will happen when it connects. So instead I jackknife and vault over the side of the pickup. It rocks as her boot dents the panel.

And we are right back where we started, with me scrabbling away from her in the dark on the gritty floor of the warehouse.

But this time the dark is my friend. In fact, I wouldn't really have said the place is dark at all, not compared to the Pit. A thin crack of light shows from under the rollup door. Blinks of light lance down from the rooms upstairs, muted through grimy windows, but as bright as Heaven to me. I have no trouble at all seeing where I was going.

And I know the warehouse. I have been living here for years now, spending sometimes months essentially alone, exploring, mapping, searching, and I know the floor of the warehouse better than I know my own face.

I am older and stronger, too, and I have used my last few months to build up both musculature and endurance, anticipating that one day I might be glad of them.

None of it is going to matter. I can see it instantly. Goldie isn't human, someone or something that can be fought. She is feral, elemental, a force beyond muscle and bone and relentless as an incoming thunderstorm. If I stay and fight, I will lose. And this time it won't be a beating. She'll take an arm. A leg, maybe. I'll be back in the Pit, with a chain on my neck.

Well, Hell.

I do the only thing I can think of to do. I bolt up the stairs.

Now, in every horror film—and I've seen them all, believe me—the worst possible thing you can do is run *up* a building when the bad guy is chasing you. You eventually run out of up and then there's nowhere to go. But in the moment I catch hold of the relative safety and familiarity of my cell and I want to be back there. Maybe, I think as I run up the clanging steps, I can bolt the door. Brace it with something.

Long enough to get my secret weapon.

I can hear her coming up behind me, and in my mind she soars up five steps to my one. I can feel the hot breath on my neck. Any second her claw will grasp my arm and fling me like a used rag into the echoing space of the open warehouse.

But I make it to my room. I slam the door and throw myself on my cot and reach underneath for the one, last chance I have.

My fingers close on nothing but rotting burlap.

It's gone. My secret. My one possible weapon.

The door crashes open, slamming against the wall and rebounding against Goldie's implacable frame. She stalks in, face a mask, eyes dead as a shark's, hands curled like the talons of a great killing bird.

I take up the cot like a shield, but she tears it from my grasp as easily as one rips a poster from the wall. I try some of the poses I learned from the Internet, but some things you can't learn from a screen, and she batted my feeble attempts away, clamps an iron hand on my neck, and squeezes.

I drop straight down to the floor.

Some things you *can* learn from a screen. One of them is that unless you're an Olympic gymnast, or Darth Vader, you can't hold the dead weight of a human in a straight-arm grip. Her small hand loses purchase and I thump to the concrete.

It buys me little time. There is nowhere to go. But one other thing I learned is that a *little* time is more than *no* time.

It buys me a second. Two. A splitfractured moment for a miracle to occur, if it wants to.

It wants to.

Goldie convulses, her eyes rolling back in her head, and she shudders like a leaf in the storms of autumn. Then she falls limp and boneless at my feet.

"I couldn't do it while she was touching you," Katulka says, holding the DIY taser I'd lovingly spliced together over the last month from parts in the barrels below.

I glare at her accusingly. "You weren't supposed to do it at all. That was my job."

She shrugs. "You couldn't have. It had to be me."

#

I pick the lock on Goldie's door. Learned from YouTube, never successfully executed until that day.

The treasure room is about half full with sacks of money, just like in the cartoons. Stacks of tens and twenties, a few fifties, some hundreds. We take a lot of them, slinging them two and three at a time over our shoulders and lugging them to the pickup.

Intermittently, we sort of talk.

"How did you find the taser?"

"In your room? Where else could you hide it?"

"Why are you here?"

"They called me to come get you, then called and said never mind. That's when I knew."

"Knew what?"

"That you were finally alive."

"I've been alive for years."

She just laughs, not mockingly, not sadly, just...laughs. Maybe it's joy. That's something I have to learn about myself.

I couldn't just run. I would never have made it out. But I could *drive*. Well, I could have Katulka drive, just as I pictured it those months ago when for a lost and careless moment Goldie gave the idea to Katulka, who gave it to me. Without her, I could not have left. Without me, she could not have run. But together, by morning we're two states away in front of a cash-preferred motel outside a blue-collar city.

She leans her head forward, touching the steering wheel. I want to reach out and run a finger along the perfect curve of her neck. She breathes in, breathes out, breathes in, breathes out. She turns her head toward me, and the one side of her mouth tugs upward, just a little.

I didn't need a video to teach me what to do about that.

A Butterfly's Bite

Beck Hiatt

The *Château de Beau,* playground of the rich and famous, was not so different from home, Alexander thought.

He woke up at 7 in the morning, wide awake on the dot as usual. He grabbed and thoroughly inspected the handgun under his pillow before walking past the bathroom to the mini-kitchen. He prepared a sandwich of dry bread and a tasteless paste he produced from a bag sitting on the counter. After preparing and eating his breakfast he went into the bathroom, casting a wary eye around it before entering. He took a quick cold shower, relieved himself, and brushed his teeth.

He opened a briefcase which sat next to the sink, revealing a bundle of well packed clothes and a variety of pockets filled with implements, ranging from a small camera to bandages to wire clippers to hand spikes for climbing walls. He pulled out and put on a suit, cinching the perfect knot in his tie. Then he pulled a beard and several other makeup tools from the pockets in his case. In mere minutes he looked nothing like the clearly English Alexander Moriano Smith the Third, his thin face, sharp carved cheekbones, short blonde hair, and cold blue eyes replaced by an old man who had smiled too much in his lifetime, with a gray beard and a balding head, the perfect touches.

Before Alexander left the room he took one more thing from his case, his favorite weapon, its once gleaming metal blade dulled save for the cutting edge which shone like a mirror. Slipping the implement into a hidden pocket and picking up the briefcase he walked to the window one last time before vaulting the low sill dropping onto the twelfth-floor fire escape.

He walked through the car packed-streets at a determined pace, pretending to admire the short yellow brick buildings until he seemingly casually came across the *L'atelier du Jardin,* a simple restaurant that disguised itself as somewhere much greater. Inside he sat himself at a table near a window and ordered an unimpressive meal, a buttered croissant and a glass of water, and then he waited. As he watched he saw many interesting and flamboyant characters cross in front of the establishment- a man with three hats on his head, a beggar, a mime, a woman and her child, a pompous and large man who appeared to be American, and hordes of tourists –yet he was watching for none of these people.

Finally, precisely at nine, the individual he sought, a young man in a sharp suit and bowler, walked into the restaurant. Alexander smiled. The mark was indeed predictable; he would fall easily to his plans.

The man ordered an egg, bacon, and toast with a cup of coffee, exactly what he always ordered, and sat at the table directly in front of Alexander's, where he always sat. He finished his meal in exactly 30 minutes and left the restaurant, leaving a sizable tip. Alexander waited just a few moments before he too got up and left.

Alexander followed the man from a distance, keeping his head down so it would never seem as though he was following him. The young man finally turned into a poorly lit alleyway, looking left and right with a degree of caution not previously shown in his confident air. Alexander closed the distance carefully, hugging the wall to avoid the man's awareness. For this was the one variable part of the man's day, where he parked.

Stalking him carefully down this little traveled street he slowly pulled the knife from the hidden pocket of his suit. The man finally came to his car, opened the door slowly and did exactly what the spy expected him to do–stuck his hand in the back and fiddled with a safe built into the middle seat. His habitual caution lapsed, as normally he would now be under the watchful supervision of exactly seven guards: two in cars, three watching every entrance to this location, and two men–

including his long-trusted friend, Jarvis–who should have been watching his every move from a van down the street.

Unfortunately for him, they were all in the wrong place; their orders, intercepted by Alex, had told them to watch an identical white car halfway across Paris. Well, except Jarvis.

The man seemed satisfied that nothing had been moved within the safe so he reached back to lock it again. But he stopped, his hand stalling before falling to the seat. Collapsing on the ground he could see a man in a suit standing over him, a bloody butterfly knife in hand.

"I never was on your side," Alexander whispered.

"Jarvis? Why?" And with that the young man dropped dead, as his blood slowly pooled around him.

Quickly Alexander reached into the car, grabbing the contents of the safe, a bundle of loose papers. Alexander raised an eyebrow. "This was his prized secret?" He sneered. "A foolish thing to die for."

Then, scoffing at the predictability of the British, he reversed his jacket, pulled off his disguise and walked away.

\#

When Alexander disembarked from the plane, he was long gone from the scene of the crime, in fact in the JFK airport all the way in the States. He grabbed his bags and briskly walked through the building, and he was out in the cold winter air. A sharp wind whipped across the streets beneath a cold gray sky. A short ride later he found himself standing outside a large, bland, brick of a building, its sole remarkable features being silvery windows and a large glass door. Walking in he once again found himself in the dry and tasteless lobby of the towering structure. The receptionist didn't even look up from her phone as he went directly to the elevator. He pressed the button for the seventh floor, and patiently waited.

When the doors opened he was met by two large men in wrinkly suits. "Come with us."

Alexander sighed. "Very well."

They led him into a room where sat a man, more wrinkled than his guards' suits, and more gray than the building itself, sitting behind a mahogany desk with ornate decoration. He shuffled some papers for a moment before he looked up and said, "Yes, Alex?"

"I retrieved the file you requested."

"Th-the Atombanane? I never would have expected you to, to come so quickly."

Alexander proffered him the folder which the man seemed all too eager to take hold of. Yet Alex held his grip. "The money." the man seemed taken aback by his directness. "Why, why of course" he gave a weak smile, his hands reaching under the table.

"Don't." Alex's forceful tone stopped him, and he begrudgingly surrendered, pulling out a handgun, which he placed on the desk, and a suitcase, which when opened revealed a large quantity of money. "Very well." Alex relinquished the papers into the man's hands, grabbed the briefcase, and backing away grabbed a knife from one of the bodyguards' hands, throwing it onto the man's desk. "I thought you more, honorable." While his former client looked down in disbelief he promptly left.

Back on the street he checked his flip phone, too many missed messages. He started by deleting the multitude of false leads, one from India, to shady. One from D.C. oh heavens no. One from somewhere in Michigan, yet another death threat. Yet another message from his landlord about potential eviction. One from New Mexico almost certainly for someone lesser. But wait, the New Mexico one, he paused and read the digits, by all normal assumptions it was a normal 10 digit phone number, but with a quadruple 0, this one could be serious.

Ultimately after going back and forth in his mind, he decided it wouldn't hurt to listen to the message. "*Hey, Yeah, I know who you are. And guess what! I got a job, for you, that needs you. I need you, I wouldn't trust anyone else with this work. You worked with Michael Star, I'm the one who made his career.-*" Alex paused the audio, Michael Star, he hadn't worked with Star since he blew up in Afghanistan, their last mission as a team still haunted him. It had been 20 years ago and he hadn't worked with anyone else since. In fact he had made it a point to block out all memories of his former friend, but now he needed to remember. Who had he said he worked for? Antonio Houstann, that was it, a thin Texan he had said, and a ruthless businessman.

He unpaused the audio. "*The name's Houstann, and if yall are interested in, say 30 million dollars, come on out to the west, and it'll be worth your time."* There was an audible click, as the message ended.

30 Million dollars?!? Alex knew more than most people what it would take to get ANYBODY to shell out that kind of cash, even this job had only netted him a few hundred thousand dollars, and he felt he was paid quite well. With 30 million he could finally retire–to a mansion–and still have plenty to spare, this may have been the break he was looking for! Quickly he made calls, canceling his appointments, and telling the clients he had lined up to find a new hitman till further notice. Then quickly he grabbed a new cab, straight back to the airport, where he paid for an airplane ticket to New Mexico.

#

When he landed he was disappointed to find New Mexico was still in the middle of the desert. It didn't matter how much he was being paid, he still detested these sandy rocky landscapes. He dialed Houstann's number, it rang for nearly no time, before that same heavy Texas accent came out the speaker, *"Alex! Glad to see you gave me a call! Tell me where're you at?"*

"I'm at the San Luis airport--"

"Say No More! I'll be there within the hour! Just hang tight!" There was yet another loud click as Alex resigned himself to waiting for this over-exuberant potential employer to arrive.

To pass the time he found himself at a table in a hotel lobby near the airport, flipping through a tourist guide to the state, dry, dry, sand, more dry. It was frankly one of the most boring places he had ever been, he was used to lavish locations, 5 star hotels and expensive food, not hole in the wall deserts without proper amenities. Even as he sneered at the pathetic excuses for tourist destinations a vehicle screeched into the parking lot, going faster than it certainly should've been. It was a golden limousine with whitewashed tires and a shining golden eagle for a hood ornament.

Alex apprehensively watched as a man, wearing cowboy garb, gilded with golden trim, a 10 gallon hat perched on his head like a cat. He was a thinner man with deep creases and smile lines on his face, which was adorned by a waxed mustache that gave his expression a peculiar grin. He spotted Alex behind the window and threw his arms wide before running towards him and into the building, "Alex! I knew I could count on y'all!"

He extended his hand. Alex didn't move to grab it, "Paranoid? Don't worry! So is everyone else!" He retracted his hand. "Anyway, come on!"

Alex didn't follow. "We have time to discuss the details right here."

Houstann slumped over. "Come on Alex, I'm risking my neck being out here, can'tcha trust me?"

"With 30 million on the line? I trust nobody."

"Fair enough" he sat down at the table with Alex.

"I need you to help me with business matters–"

"Not a businessman." Alex leaned back in his chair.

"No, but trust me you can help. A lot."

"What use do you have for a contract killer in–" he gestured vaguely, "'business' matters."

He leaned in closer to Alex. "I got a project going on to redirect a river for one of the big cities out here, it's worth almost 100 million dollars."

"I still fail to comprehend what use you have for me," he said, "if you already HAVE the contract."

"Yes, well I ain't done, there's a group of, uh, extremists, who've been trying to blow up my progress for months now."

"And you want me to kill their leader?"

"Precisely."

"Very well."

"Great!" Houstann shot up like a rocket. "Let's get back to HQ and we can iron out a plan there!"

Alex stood up slowly following the brash Texan to his car. "I'll even let you ride shotgun!" Houstann exploded at his own joke, still chuckling even as Alex slid into the seat rubbing his brow.

\#

It seemed to Alex like they had been driving by the same river, passing mesas and canyons, for hours when suddenly while going through one of these canyons, they turned sharply into a dark cave that could have fit a car much larger than the one they were in. Houstann winked at Alex. "It's underground, I don't reckon they found it yet."

Even as he said it the sides of the tunnel seemed to smooth, slowly lights began appearing on the walls in regular fashion, revealing painted stripes on what was clearly concrete, Alex marveled at how smoothly the base was integrated into its surroundings. After about a minute of driving through the cave base they came to a large metal door. Houstann pressed a button on the dash. In response red lights on the walls began to flash. A klaxon sounded and the door slowly ground open.

Alex looked around in alarm. Houstann chuckled. They drove through into a much brighter lit concrete hallway, lined with various vehicles, vans, cars, a tank. They passed all of it, leaving the closing door behind them, and came to an empty parking spot along the wall, which Houstann pulled his car into.

As they got out, a young man with strangely familiar black hair and green eyes, who could have been in his early 20s but carried himself like a teenager strolled over to them.

"You hadda pick up this loser?" He said, gesturing in the direction of Alex.

"Who might this child be?" Alex asked Houstann.

"What, CHILD?! I'm notta kid!" He nearly had his finger up Alex's nose. Houstann let out a great roar of a laugh.

"Y'all knuckleheads took it 'bout as well as I expected." Smiling to himself he explained, "Alex, you're going to work with Jeffrey Smith, you get to be in charge, but he needs experience, and I need you to teach him a thing or two."

"I did not sign up just to be a babysitter!"

"I'M NOT A FREAKIN' BABY!!"

"Shut up you overgrown infant."

"OR AN INF–"

Houstann cut him off, his smile wearing down. "Be quiet won't you, and hear it out," he said before clearing his throat, "I need you to work together, and if either of you back out you won't get paid." He looked directly at Alex. "I'll even be a little generous if you could show him the ropes. Say $10 mil on top of our current agreement."

Alex paused, mulling it over.

"If he won't take it, I will!" Alex glared in Jeffrey's direction.

Alex massaged his face with his hands. "Fine."

Houstann's smile reappeared. "Good! Let's get you guys oriented."

Houstann led them through a door near his car into a much more human sized hallway. There were painted stripes along the walls and a quick glance through the window on the many doorways along the walls revealed rooms with hundreds, nay thousands of filing cabinets and giant blocky computers. "Impressed? We practically built our own internet down here."

Alex nodded though his face masked his surprise, he hadn't thought the 'internet' was that big a deal, Houstann clearly thought differently.

Eventually they came to a set of stairs, which Houstann led them up. There were a lot of stairs. When at last they reached the top Houstann stopped to catch his breath before leading them through one more door where they arrived in the command center. It was huge, sleek, and impressive. Massive steel buttresses reached from floor to ceiling, the walls were covered in panels of lights, signs, and decorated simply with red striping. A large digital clock rested high on the back wall. In between the walls were rows upon rows of boxy computers, each had a person working behind it, paying no attention to the group that had just arrived, but the far greatest part of the whole thing was the view, for the final wall was that of a floor to ceiling window, spanning the entirety of the room and looking out high above the ground.

Alex failed to mask his amazement as Jeffrey jeered. "Never been up this high, old man?"

Alex shot back, "It must be truly extraordinary from your hei—"

Houstann waved his hand to stop him. "Over there's the dam." He pointed and they looked to see a massive concrete structure being erected, nearly done actually, at a river coming out below them. "When that baby is all dammed up it'll be making me a hundred billion dollars a year."

"When is it done?" Houstann looked nervous at Alex's comment.

"Well, should be done midway through next month, but I'm worried he'll hit before then. It's probly 'bout time I told you what you're here for."

Alex rubbed his hands together. "Finally."

"HA! you look like a squirrel" Jeffrey chuckled.

Houstann shook his head before leading them to a table in the center of the room. On the way Alex swiped a paper with the plan for the dam on it off the top of a computer. Tucking it in his suit for later. Sitting at the table Houstann finally let them in on the mission.

"I brought you here to do one thing, kill my brother." Alex and Jeffrey fell silent while he breathed in. "Ever since we were kids, he's only ever made it his mission to break what I build. I build a block tower, he knocks it down, I found a company, he exposes quote *'unfavorable'* business practices to the press. I thought I had finally left him behind when I got him thrown in federal prison, but of course not! Not only does he get out, but the first thing he does is try and BLOW UP MY STUFF!" The table shook with the force of Houstann's fist. "Needless to say, I'm tired of his antics and I think I finally decided he's gonna die, which is where y'all come in."

Alex leaned forwards pressing his fingers against each other, Jeffrey mimicked him, but exaggerated and with a goofy expression which Alex tried to ignore. "I don't know where he is, but you HAVE to find and kill that idiot, no good excuse for a genetic twin, got it?"

Alex nodded his head. "Of cou–"

"Don't worry I got this." Jeffrey leaned back and put his feet on the table.

Alex frowned. "Under normal circumstances I would guarantee success, but, if I have to drag this cretin around I fail to be so optimistic."

"Tough luck chucklehead, you wish you had these guns." Jeffrey flexed his arms, which only showed how scrawny he really was.

Houstann put a hand on his head and sighed. "Think you can do it? Or do I need to get somebody else?"

Alex looked him directly in the eyes. "He will die."

Houstann brightened up considerably. "Good! I'll be happy to provide y'all with whatever you need, guns, cars, lethal substances, just tell me."

Alex cocked his head slightly. "Some sort of low-profile vehicle would be satisfactory."

Jeffrey opened his mouth but was interrupted by Alex. "Ignore him, we just need the car." Getting up he quickly fell in line behind Houstann while Jeffrey gaped at his retreating backside.

\#

Jeffrey sat slumped over in the passenger seat of the rectangular Buick Roadmaster Houstann had lent them. Alex kept his eyes on the road. There was no conversation between the two of them.

Slowly Jeffrey turned to face Alex. "Where are we going, anyway?"

Alex sighed. "A town about twenty miles this way, Houstann said it may have clues as to the whereabouts of our target."

"Hmph." He turned away again.

"Why didn't ya ask for any guns?"

"I don't need any more tools than the ones on my body."

"Whada 'bout me?"

"What about you?" Alex glanced at Jeffrey, raising an eyebrow.

"The big man said you'd teach me a thing or two."

Alex rolled his eyes. "Thing one, never work with a partner."

"Oh come on, that sucks!"

"It will save you a lot of mourning."

"What?"

"Nevermind, it's too complicated for your brain to—" he paused to maneuver around a pothole, "—understand."

"Are you always this rude?"

"Are you always this stupid?"

Jeffrey turned away from Alex again.

Alex exhaled, time to earn his extra ten million. "Who are you?"

"What? Ya heard the Big guy right? The name's Jeffrey."

"Yes of course I know your name, but who are you?

Jeffrey glared at him. "I don't wanna talk."

"Very well."

Alex swerved hard to avoid yet another pothole in the road. They drove past a sign that so kindly informed them they had another fifteen miles to go.

Jeremy groaned. "Fifteen miles!? Stuck in here with you!?"

Alex turned to retort when the car's windshield shattered. A bullet ripped through the back. The car swerved. Alex barely managed to keep it under his control. An explosion barely missed the crippled vehicle, opening a gash in the pavement. The car fell to its side, sliding a good few meters before it fell back to its original footing, spun completely backwards.

Alex's shaky hands pulled a gun from an inside pocket. Another bullet shattered the driver's window, spraying his face with glass.

He kicked the car door open, and stumbled out; his left leg failed him, bending under the pressure.

He looked up. A man in a black mask stood on a hill, a rocket launcher raised in his arms, Alex had no hope of victory. He turned his head as if to aim. A gunshot. The rocketeer slumped over dead. Alex looked around for a savior. A man walked over to him. He couldn't have put up a fight if he tried. The man took off Alex's suit coat and poked the bloodier parts around a bit, before grabbing a stick for his leg, and bandaging up his wounds. He walked to the other side of the car, where he did the same for Jeffrey, pulling him out onto the street first. Alex was conscious for only a few more moments before he succumbed to blood loss and exhaustion, and passed out.

\#

When next he woke up, he found himself in a clean room with fading wallpaper, lying on a sepia couch printed with flowers. It was rather clean with only a stack of newspapers and a pair of crutches lying in the corner. A few furnishings adorned the room, a grandfather clock and a large armchair. He waited a moment before he tried to sit up. Pain shot through his left leg and up his spine; a grunt escaped his lips. Though he tried, the pain became too much for his body which seemed to forcibly push him down.

Reluctantly, he obeyed its wishes, but did not quit. He looked around hoping for something, anything, to help him get up. Craning his neck back he saw an ornate lamp. He reached up, ignoring the increase in physical discomfort, and grabbed the shining brass base of the light. He swung it around, placing it on the ground to use as a sort of makeshift crutch to aid him in getting up, and promptly fell off the couch with a thud. As he tried to push himself up, he heard footsteps.

A man spoke. "Ho Ho, you got yourself in a pickle right now!"

Alex fumed, pulling himself up as best he could. "What is th—Gah!" He fell to his face again. The same man who had saved Alex picked him up and put him back on the couch, this time sitting up with his left leg in a splint propped up by the lamp. Now that Alex could see him, he observed the man's wrinkled face, clearly wizened by years. "You got off lucky, you might just be sore! Ain't that dandy."

Alex glared, trying to recollect himself to reply.

"For all the blood you were in." The man shuffled about. "What's your name anyhow?"

"Alex." Alex waved his hand limply and carefully leaned over. "Enough, what do you want?" his hand dropped to his leg while the other man recoiled.

"Why you act like nobody's ever done something kind for kind's sake for you in your life!"

"They generally don't."

"Well that's a darn shame, guess I should set an example shouldn't I."

Alex rolled his eyes.

Unprompted, the man continued. "What brought you out here anyway?" He raised an eyebrow. "Law trouble?"

Alex shook his head.

"Whatever it may be, don't sweat it, I won't tell nobody." He gave a little devilish grin. "Care for a drink, Alex?"

Alex ignored the question. "Where is Jeffrey?"

The man cocked his head.

"The kid," Alexander said, gesturing with his hands.

"Oh! He's fine, you'll see him running again in a week or two. The two of you got lucky!"

Alex nodded his head slightly. He moved again to get up, balancing himself on his splint. The old man grabbed a crutch and handed it to him. Alex hesitated before grabbing it, taking the weight off his wounds. The old man looked at him expectantly.

Alex frowned. "What?"

"How about a thank you."

Alex gritted his teeth. "Thanks," he said, before hobbling to the door frame.

"Where're you headed?"

Alex didn't answer, he looked around and saw a door that was somewhat less plain than the rest of the building. He stumbled as quickly as he could to the door, opened it, and burst out into the warm afternoon sun. He stopped on a wooden porch, attached to a house with a suntanned white paint job that was peeling in large areas.

The house sat on a dusty road that was more tar than street, flanked by buildings that largely looked like much the same structure but shoved in many shapes and sizes. The most surprising part was the angry mob outside the house.

He heard footsteps behind him, before the old man pushed past him, his brow furrowed, shadowing his eyes. "What are you doin' here!?" he called out to the mob.

A man stepped out of the group, a portly fellow with balding hair, and a glossy white sash draped across his wrinkled suit. "I, the Mayor, and we, the people of Sinival, demand the traitors you harbor for a fair, but mostly speedy trial!" The shouts of agreement from the small crowd echoed their approval.

"Look, you can't have him now, I know you're tired of the whole thing, but you gotta give 'im a chance." He looked directly in the mayor's eyes, before quietly to the group. "You let *me* stay." That seemed to quiet the mob.

"Mr. Falks er, Edward, I value your opinion, but nevertheless I must satisfy the demands of justice! This criminal is part of the debauchery that has so plagued our lovely establishment. We MUST bring him in."

The mob cheered, pressing forward to get past Edward.

"STOP!" Edward roared, flailing his arms about, "give me some time, please! At least so he can heal!"

Alex backed away from the running group, slamming the door behind him. Through the wooden planks he heard the cacophony of slamming feet stop. There was a flurry of muffled talking, followed by a multitude of groans. The porch creaked.

The door opened and Edward walked in, a dark look on his face. "I got you a month."

"Why? How?"

"Are you gonna argue?" He stalked past Alex.

"Who are you?"

Edward looked back at Alex. "Edward Falks, I'll tell ya more later."

#

Later turned out to be just a few hours when Edward called Alex into his backyard. He stood in what existed of the dry yellow grass next to an old tarp-covered car, which had its engine strewn in maybe 50 parts on the ground. "Alex, you wouldn't mind giving me a hand with this, wouldya?"

If it weren't for having nothing more to do Alex might have said no, but he decided to take the chance. "With what?"

Edward tapped a wrench against what remained of the car's internals. "I'm gettin too old, I can't get this bolt anymore."

Alex hobbled over, propping himself on the protruding headlight casing. He took the wrench from Edward and leaned over to see the troublesome screw. He saw it wedged underneath the edge of the siding, attached to a strangely familiar device, or one might say weapon, positioned behind the headlight. As he finished it dawned on him that his savior might be more than he let on. "Where did you get this car?"

Edward chuckled. "I bought this car back in '46, been keeping it in decent condition since."

An outlandish thought began to dawn on Alex. "Falks. Falks, I know you. You're the Ducky Shincracker!"

He sighed. "I hate that name, it's been quite some time since I even heard it." He smiled. "But's nice to know I ain't been forgotten."

"They say you died 20 years ago!"

"That's what they thought, it would be what they were told."

"You faked your death?"

"Not quite, but if you'll be willing to wait a while, I might afford you my story."

"Nothing more?"

Edward laughed. "Well, if you insist." he ripped the tarp off the car, which was in fact the famous spy's even more famous car, The Killer Diller. Its sleek round body shone in the noon sunlight.

Alex could only stare, his uncontrollable admiration showing through his normally airtight persona.

"Isn't she a beauty?"

Alex nodded before turning to the spy, thought long dead. "How are you alive?"

Edward smirked. "It'd be a bit of a tale, but, sometime, I'll tell you how I got here. I think you'd understand I don't want to go blabbing bout' that to any old soul."

Alex nodded his head, he had a point. Through the rest of the day, Alex continued to work on the gleaming machine with Edward, peppering him with questions all the while. In fact long into the evening they sat there. Edward answered fewer of Alex's questions than he had hoped, but at least he didn't pry too much in return.

#

As the month went by Alex's leg healed to the point he could walk without a splint or crutch. Jeffrey was not so lucky and had been bedridden by his injuries ever since the accident. It was not with shame Alex confessed he hadn't even truly been to see him, Edward on the other hand spent long hours in his room listening to him talk. And it was here that Alex would eavesdrop on their conversations. Nearly halfway through the month, as Edward went to care for the boy, Alex crept through the hallway, stopping by the door where he crouched down to listen through the nearly closed door.

In truth, he was hoping for any confirmation that Jeffrey was fit enough to walk. The kid was the only thing holding Alex here, and he desperately wanted to leave this leg of their mission behind.

"I brought you some soup, it's nice and warm!"

"Thanks Eddie."

Alex detested the nickname for such a prestigious individual.

"You're welcome son." Edwards' voice paused. "What's troublin' you?"

"Alex."

The bed creaked before Edward spoke again. "He's a hard man, isn't he?"

"But why? Why does he hate me?"

"I don't know. Maybe he's just not ready."

"I just wish, I just wish he could be more like a dad."

"Like your father?"

"Na, I never knew mine." He chuckled. "But you knew that already."

That line made Alex take a step back, it may have seemed out of place, but he could remember now as clear as day. Black hair, green eyes, 'But you knew that already'.

A chill shot through Alex's spine as he backed away from the open door. It wasn't possible, no it couldn't be. Yet he had never thought the Ducky Shincracker would be alive, and he was in his house! Alex quietly rushed to the living room, he grabbed Edward's home phone and dialed Houstann's number, adding a special code to the end as a password.

After ringing a few times Houstann picked up. *"Alex! Got some good news for me?"*

"No, I don't have too much time to talk, I need you to tell me everything you know about Jeffrey." *"Everything?! Why do y'all even care? I thought ya hated the kid!"*

"Tell me."

"Fine. I can tell y'all what I know." There was a pause of a few moments while he rustled through some paper, *"Alright, let's see now. He comes from Boston. He likes peanut butter sandwiches, despises jelly. Went to English Hi–"*

"Do you have his parents' names?" Alex clenched his fist around the phone.

"Um, Maybe, let's see, Ah yes it's right here. No name for the dad, the mothers name is, Emmeline Smith." Alex's knuckles were white from holding the phone so tight, his eyes were wide open, and he struggled to find words to speak.

"Anything else Alex?"

Alex shook his head before rapidly speaking into the phone. "No, that will be all." He didn't wait for a reply before setting the phone down gingerly, and sitting down on the couch. His breathing was heavy, his blood ran cold. It seemed to him that though he had tried to bury the past behind him, it was quickly resurfacing where he would least expect it. It couldn't be possible, surely, but who else was named Emmeline Smith, green eyes, black hair. No, there could be no doubt about it. Troubled, he retired to the bed Edward had loaned him, falling into a fitful sleep.

#

The next day he wanted answers. He ran into Edward in the hall, the only other individual he had ever met who woke up at the same time as he did. "Today, you will tell me how you survived."

Edward looked him in the eyes, before nodding his head. "Yes, I reckon it's about time. Come on, let's go in here."

He walked into the living room, gesturing at the couch for Alex, before sitting in the chair. "Let me see, where should I begin? You already know my legacy, so I s'pose I'll start at the beginin' of my final mission." Alex nodded, his attention locked on Edward. "I arrived in the Killer Diller, drove right into a big huge garage, I must say I was rather impressed. I was going to meet a man named Roberto, no one knew me by that name, but I had a laugh that we shared a last name."

"Wait, Roberto? What was the last name?"

"Please don't interrupt, but I'll tell you his name was Houstann."

Alex swallowed.

"Anyway," Edward went on, "he had a lucrative opportunity for me, he offered me a hefty sum of a few million dollars, for one very specific job. To kill his brother. You see I did a bit of snoopin' before I left, and I was talking around, and it sure as hell didn't start then, that war had been going for years best I could tell. There was one extra requirement, however, I was a contract man, and I didn't care much for sticking around with a single employer. I saw too many good friends die when they got settled down. But this man said that was perfectly fine, so long as I agreed to train someone who would. A spy who could stick about and do his dirty work. So he introduced me to a young man named Micheal Star."

Alex sat up straighter. "You worked with Micheal? But he never mentioned you!"

Edward nodded. "It's good to know you met 'im. He was a good man, and it's good to know he keeps my secret. But anyways, he introduced me to Micheal Star. My mission was to show 'im the ropes of the trade and give him some much-needed pointers on the art of our craft. Unfortunately we got along pretty poorly, I didn't much like him and I thought he thought vice versa.

We ended up in this empty place when we were approached by a soldier, who claimed to be from Roberto's brother, Antonio. We had 'im in a pickle pretty quick, but turned out he just had a counteroffer, Antonio was promising double whatever Roberto was paying us, if we would merely turn traitor and kill Roberto instead. How he knew we were about I had no idea, but I wasn't 'bought to take any chances. I figured it was a trap, and told Star as such, but before I could drill the soldier farther I found myself knocked cold by my own apprentice.

When I came too I was alone, the soldier was gone, Star was gone, and he had taken my weapons too, even some I was sure he hadn't known about. I had to keep going, no matter how bleak the prospect was, the Ducky Shincracker had never failed, and I wasn't about to tarnish my golden reputation now.

But alas even as I walked back to this very town, a car pulled up. A fancy American deal, new age muscle car. Out stepped Star, with a gun pointed at my chest. *"Well it finally came to this, the teacher was upended by the apprentice, and now I've come to give Antonio peace of mind."*

I hung my head, I was beat, and I was prepared to die. Even as I prepared to meet his bullets, it was soft words, not gunshots, which caught my ears. *"But I figure what Antonio doesn't know won't kill him, and I can't kill you. Goodbye friend, goodbye."*

I could hardly believe my ears, I had just been spared. I think that was the first true kindness I had ever known all my life, or at least for much of it that I could remember. And that kindness changed me, I went from cold-blooded killer to small town softie just like that." Edward snapped his fingers. "And now you find me here, a changed man."

Alex sat stunned at the retelling of Edwards' story.

"I reckon, though you and Jeffrey have been pretty tight-lipped, that you're in much the same situation as I was then. And I'm here to give any help you need."

Alex looked Edward in the eyes, his mouth quivered. "I think Jeffrey may be my son."

Edward sat back. "Well, that's a doozy. Did you even know you had a son?"

"I thought he and his mother were dead." He hesitated. "When Micheal Star died."

"That's a shame. My advice, don't let it boil. Get it out as soon as you're able."

Alex nodded. "I need to complete this job."

Edward leaned forward. "Which side are you on?"

"Antonio's."

Edward leaned back again, blowing air out of his mouth. "Oh boy, that won' make you more popular 'round here."

Alex cocked his head. "Why not?"

"Why?" Edward laughed. "That great big dam of his might destroy this whole town, that's why!"

Alex still looked puzzled so Edward explained. "That water is being redirected from this town, off to some big city." He nodded his head. "Most of us have already accepted our fate, but some would shoot you where you stand for dealing with his business."

"Would you?"

Edward smiled. "I trust you Alex, I think whatever you do, you'll need to do. And maybe that dam is the only way to get these rock solid people out of the way before those two brothers blow the place to smithereens." He got up. "Come with me."

Edward led him to his bedroom, a room Alex had never been in. Clothes were strewn about, and it was packed tight with bookshelves, a wardrobe, a small bed, and a desk that was hardly visible beneath mountains of paperwork. It was to this pile he strode, throwing the papers on the floor as he went through them, till he came upon a folded up map. He spread it out on what clean surfaces remained on his bed. He pulled a pen out of his pocket and, after a moment's search, marked an X off to the west of the town. "That would be Roberto's stronghold."

Alex nodded. "This is very useful."

Edward winked. "I know, and this is a great time to show you, cause Jeffrey's well enough to get going. And you still have a week of 'healing time' before the mob shows up to take you away."

Alex nodded. "We leave tonight."

Edward was about to reply when they heard a mighty knock on the front door.

#

When the two opened the door they found the mayor once more, his suit seemed freshly ironed and his sash might have been just a tad whiter than the last time Alex had seen him "Edward, The time is up, now deliver your pris'ners into the hands of the law!"

Edward put his hands on his head, "But they still have a week!"

"I figured I'd put a stop to any of their funny business, and arrest them now when they least expect it."

"I can't let you do this."

"Step aside, Edward, unless you want to sleep on the cold stone floor of a prison cell yourself!"

Edward looked from the Mayor, to Alex, to the Mayor, to Alex. He took one last look at Alex and, as Alex dreaded, stepped aside mouthing the word, sorry. Alex could hardly believe it, this man whom he had almost begun to trust would stand aside and let Alex be carted off to death row.

A deputy seized him, Alex would normally have fought, if not for the shock at Edward's betrayal. Even as he was shoved in the backseat of a police car, he couldn't help but stare at Edward's downturned head.

#

Alex couldn't sleep. Jeffrey was trying. Alex paced around the small square stone cell occasionally pausing at the iron bars which separated him from freedom. Jeffrey lay with his eyes closed on the singular metal shelf, which was meant to be a bed but did a poor job of it.

Alex had just been through the jeers of the people, and was not in a good mood. They had been quite vocal about executing him immediately, including the mayor. It had taken the county sheriff to explain to the mob that in America, everyone gets a trial, no matter who they worked for or how surely they should die. But now it was quiet in the jailhouse, night had fallen what felt like hours ago, but Alex couldn't be sure in this monotonous place.

It tantalized him how close freedom was, just on a table across the hall lay his weapons, tools, lock picks, phone, any would have been useful now. But most importantly, he hungered for his knife. Carelessly thrown among the miscellaneous pile, he desired it above any of the other implements he was separated from, but he had to be patient, bide his time, and maybe he could get out of this. He looked at Jeffrey, his eyes were closed, but his breathing betrayed him as awake, and so Alex decided this was as good a time as ever. "Jeffrey." Jeffrey's eyes half opened, and a frown appeared on his face. "I need to tell you something."

"Who cares?"

Alex was taken aback by the response a little but decided to persevere.

"I-, did you-, who was your father?"

"I said who cares, dummy!"

"Listen to me you imbecile!"

"I DON'T FREAKIN' CARE!" Jeffrey rolled onto his other side. "Besides he left me and mom before I was born, who cares about him?"

"Jeffrey, you don't understan—"

"What don't I understand? You think you can barge in and tell me how my life went? Cause news flash, you don't know enough about my life to fill a fly."

Alex was about to try again when they heard a familiar voice. "Boys I hope you can forgive me for back there."

Alex turned to face Edward, dressed all in black. "But I figured it was the best way to bust you out of this joint." He produced a lock pick from his pocket, "I'll just say you managed to hide one of these away."

Alex was frankly speechless, He frankly had no conceivable idea why Edward would stick his neck out this far for him. Edward must have guessed Alex's thoughts because even as the lock clicked open, he spoke. "I trust you Alex."

He swung the door open. "Now you need to get out of here."

Alex sprinted to the table, grabbing his tools, gun, and knife, depositing them in many hidden pockets throughout his suit. He tossed Jeffrey a pistol, before following Edward outside. Sitting by the curb was a sleek shiny silver car–the Killer Diller.

Edward looked at Alex, grabbed his hand, and left a small brass key in his palm.

Alex took a step back. "I can't take your car."

Edward smiled before whispering, "Who cares? Every car gets rusty and falls apart someday. Let it have one more ride." He turned, "Time's gettin' short Alex, you best be off."

Before slipping off into the shadows. Alex looked at Jeffrey. "Get in the car," he said, and before anyone in the sleeping town of Sinival was any the wiser, a shining silver bullet of a vehicle sped off into the desert.

\#

The morning desert was quiet, maybe too quiet. Alex and Jeffrey crouched behind a dune, looking 100 meters or so to the west where a squat concrete block sat. It was huge, and its walls were adorned with metal doors, including two large vehicle bays. The roof was plated with battlements, a roof access, air conditioning units, and ducts. The best approach,

Alex deduced, was likely through said ducts, but he would proceed with caution.

Alex had told Jeffrey all his thoughts, but if he was honest, his mind wasn't on the task at hand. He turned, stood up, Jeffrey followed suit, Alex paused before he spoke. "Jeffrey, I need to tell you something."

Jeffrey rolled his eyes. "For the last time, I don't ca—"

Alex grabbed his arms. "Jeffrey, listen. I…I am your…" He looked down. "You are my son."

Jeffrey's jaw dropped open. "What?! You?! You left me! You abandoned mom!"

Alex gripped him harder. "You don't understand!"

"What don't I understand?!" Jeffrey tried to tear himself from Alex's grip. "I wished you were there every, single, day of my life!"

Alex opened his mouth to talk but what came out was what could only be described as a squeak. It felt like an icicle had been slid through his stomach, his grip slackened, Jeffrey broke away, still a look of horror on his face. Alex looked down, his hands fell to his gut, his precious knife still stuck in his abdomen. He fell to his knees, looking up at the blurry face of Jeffrey, before his son disappeared and everything went black.

#

He woke up in prison again. The difference being his companion. Sitting in front of him was a bald and muscular shirtless man in a bulletproof vest and cargo pants. His hand held a Glock. Alex himself had handcuffs. Both men sat on metal benches.

When the man saw Alex was awake, he pulled a walkie-talkie out of his pocket. "Boss, he's awake," he said before putting it back.

Alex looked down, his shirt was open, and he could see a scar where Jeffrey had stabbed him, he still didn't know what to think about that. What was more remarkable was that he could barely see the scarring, how had they managed that?

The cell he was in was significantly more secure than the town jail. Its black concrete walls were smooth as marble, a heavy metal door broke one wall in the enclosed space, a blinding white light emanated from the ceiling.

It took a few minutes, but soon the lock disengaged, the door swung open, and a third party entered the room. It was a man in a suit, his thin mustache, bowler, and angry furrowed eyebrows bore a close resemblance to Antonio Houstann. "Well, you came to kill me," the man said.

Alex didn't respond, sitting straight and refusing to break eye contact with, who could only be Roberto. "My name is Roberto Houstann." He waited as if wishing for a response from Alex. "I know you work for my *'brother'* Antonio." He paused again. "I misjudged you, I expected a more dangerous threat. Instead, I found you half dead out in the open."

He looked down at Alex's stab wound. "You can thank Dr. Ludvan for doing such an excellent job." He sighed, tilting his head back, and wringing his hands. "I'm going to give it to you clear, assassin, or should I say Alex. I know you're in it for the money. So I'd like to make you a counteroffer. Antonio may have made me into a bad guy, but I just want what he does, his twin's head on a platter. So I will pay you ten, no, twenty million dollars beyond whatever that lunkhead offered you." He tilted his head slightly, giving him a sadistic sort of look. "Just to kill him. And hand that unacceptable waste of a rival's company to me."

Alex didn't react.

"I'm going to stay here till you say something, or I get bored and kill you." He pulled a small handgun from his coat and leveled it at Alex's brow. "And bear in mind, I don't have a lot of patience right now."

Alex considered what to do, years of working in his business had given him the ability to think with death pointed at his face. He could accept the offer, but Roberto seemed like the kind of guy to shoot you in the back. He reminded Alex too much of himself.

He had to come to a decision; he began to nod, and he even began to speak. "Two da—" when the sound of a distant explosion rippled through the hallway. It was quickly accompanied by the lights flickering out, replaced by a low red light.

Shouting and gunshots could be heard from somewhere else in the building. Roberto sighed. "I have to take care of this Carl, watch him for a moment won't you?"

The guard stood up. "Yes, sir!" Before Roberto left the room he looked at Alex.

"Two days." And he left, not pausing to close the door.

The guard got up and looked out into the hall.

Alex saw his chance. "Excuse me," he said.

The guard began to turn around. "Wha—"

He never had a chance to finish his sentence before Alex's fist connected with his nose. The blow knocked him onto his back, falling into the hallway. Alex searched his pockets and found a set of keys–one of which fit his handcuffs–and another pocket contained a gun.

Alex had no idea where they were keeping his stuff, so he took the weapon he found on the man. He buttoned up his shirt and suit coat before stepping out into the poorly lit hallway. He took a guess and went to the right, where Roberto had gone. The building was maze-like, but luckily set up in an almost grid design which made it decently easy to navigate.

Following the sounds of fighting, and occasionally running groups of armed men, he soon found the source of the commotion. It was his son. He found him in a large, dark room filled with crates, it was lighter than the rest of the facility due to the moonlight spilling through the large smoking hole in the wall. In the center of the room stood a ring of Roberto's men, and just behind them Roberto himself.

The flashlights attached to the men's guns clearly illuminated his son standing in the center of the room, a shotgun in his hands and a pile of corpses at his feet. Roberto spoke. "You have caused me a great deal of trouble, so I won't be merciful." He began to walk away. "Shoot him."

The men raised their guns to fire, when suddenly a hailstorm of bullets rained down from above. It was enough to distract the group long enough that Jeffrey ducked, so the few who tried to shoot him missed. Alex let loose with a spray of firepower, it was enough for the remaining soldiers to move to hide behind cover, but when they looked to see who had been shooting at them, no one could be found. Not Alex, and not Jeffrey. Roberto walked out from behind a crate of his own, He looked out into the dark, before turning to his men. "He's gone, but he's on our side. Now get someone to fix up this hole."

#

Alex was not in fact gone, but pressed flat among the debris. His son was squashed uncomfortably nearby. When they heard the group of men leaving, Alex carefully motioned for them to crawl to the hole Jeffrey had made, before escaping the facility altogether. Jeffrey couldn't help himself at that point. "Where did you come from?!"

Alex looked at him. "I didn't die, but they captured me while I was unconscious, how long has it been?"

Jeffrey still looked astonished. "I mean, just a few days, but! But why'd ya come back for me?"

Alex looked him in the eyes. "Because I love you, I never abandoned you or Emmeline, I thought you were both dead. It tore my heart in two."

Tears began to come to Jeffrey's eyes.

Alex put his hand on his son's shoulder. "I am so sorry."

Jeffrey silently rushed into a hug, which Alex reciprocated. "Thanks," Jeffrey said, and paused. "Dad."

A real smile crept along Alex's face for the first time since Emmeline had died, or since he thought she had. They stood there in the desert, silent for a long time. Finally, Alex spoke. "Jeffrey, we have some work to do. But I have a plan."

Jeffrey smiled. "Let's do it."

Alex nodded. "Together." The pair walked off to where Jeffrey had parked the Killer Diller discussing Alex's plan the whole way.

#

The time had finally arrived, It was time to enact Alex's plan. He and Jeffrey drove towards the dam, stopping a few hundred feet away from a parking lot at the base of the ridge. Carefully they made their way across the cliff face, avoiding the cameras watching the lot.

When they came to the camera that watched the maintenance door adjacent to the area Alex pulled some wire clips out of his pocket. Working quickly he cut through the wires wrapped around the camera pole, there was an audible pop as the camera disabled.

Moving on to the door Jeffrey watched the road while Alex cracked the lock. It was a surprisingly complex piece so it took a few minutes, but it satisfyingly gave way and popped to the ground. Alex picked it up before opening the door and letting the two of them inside. As they moved in, Alex whispered to Jeffrey. "In and out, then on to the second brother." Jeffrey nodded in understanding.

On the inside, they found themselves in a low-ceilinged corridor flanked on either side by pipes of varying sizes. At regular intervals along the sides there were doors which were the best lit areas in the entire hall. Moving along they looked in a few, they were following the blueprint Alex had stolen, but it still didn't hurt to look around.

The rooms were all tight, cramped, and filled with stuff, and Alex couldn't help but reflect on the fact that this was the ugly underbelly to Houstann's beautiful HQ. As Jeffrey looked in the 8th door he had peeked in and saw just more of the same Alex spoke. "Come on, we have to move!" Jeffrey nodded his head in agreement, running to catch up with him.

Eventually they found themselves at the end where a set of stairs led up to more levels. Climbing up, Alex read the door labels. *Maintenance No.2, Maintenance No.3, Maintenance No.4, Turbines No.1, Turbines No.2.* There were an awful lot of floors to what was basically a glorified warehouse wall. As they walked, Alex asked a question that had been on his mind. "Jeffrey? Is your mother alive?" Alex whispered.

"No, she died when I was ten. I really miss her," Jeffrey responded.

"I'm so sorry to hear that." They fell back to silence once more. When they finally came to the floor they had been looking for, Alex stopped for a moment, so Jeffrey could catch up. It read *Armory.* Alex opened the door and the pair quickly slipped through, into a room filled with guns. The ceilings must have been 10 feet tall, and weapon racks extended all the way to the very top, Jeffrey couldn't believe his eyes. "OH MY GUNS! I have never seen such a beautiful room in my WHOLE life!"

Alex chuckled. "You haven't seen anything yet."

"How many guns have *you* seen?!"

"A lot more. Now let's get to work" Alex and Jeffrey pulled out packs of explosives they had found in the Killer Diller, distributing them around the room, under grenades, around boxes of C4, in bazooka barrels. They also found more in the room, and placed those carefully enough that they could create chain reactions to other parts of the room.

As they worked it was Jeffrey's turn to ask a question. "How did you meet my mom?"

Alex stopped what he was doing and looked at him. "Those are memories I tried to forget."

"Too painful?" Jeffrey asked. Alex nodded.

"But I can say Emmeline was the most beautiful, most intelligent, and most kind woman I had ever met." An edge of sadness came into his voice. "I said goodbye to Micheal Starr and to the life of a spy, but they still threatened you two. I tried to rescue you, but all I found was the smoking rubble of our home."

Jeffrey had stopped. "That's horrible!"

They were done with rigging the place to blow, as they began to leave Alex continued.

"It didn't help that a month later I learned Starr blew up in Afghanistan."

"And I do apologize for that Alex," said a deep Texan voice. A gunshot. Jeffrey fell over in pain.

Alex rushed to his side. "OW OW OW OW OW!" Jeffrey whimpered.

Alex took a bandage out of his pocket to roughly hold the wound shut. He looked in Antonio's direction, sending him a scathing look.

"Look Alex, I'm feeling a bit betrayed by y'all here."

"Likewise. You never told me this dam would kill off a whole town."

Houstann looked absolutely confused. "You? The Afghan Terror? Suddenly gettin' all idealistic on me?"

Alex just glared. Houstann sighed. "Well I am going to have to kill y'all, but I suppose you can at least see something nice before you die." Houstann walked out, and two armed guards walked in to escort Alex and Jeffrey. They led them to the Dam's control room, which was similar but not identical to his other command center. Before he had his Guards throw them on the floor, Alex stumbled to his feet. "You killed Micheal."

Houstann chuckled. "'Course I did Alex, I was the one who orchestrated the whole thing! I never meant for your wife to die, but Starr knew too much! You're lucky he never told y'all nothing more than he was told to."

Alex started but stopped when the guards raised their guns. "Was it all a lie then?! Was he ever my friend?!"

"Of course he was, you half-cocked twit! That's why I had to dispose of him!"

It was then, just as Alex was about to yell some more that they heard muffled shooting, and then the door opened. Standing in the doorway was Roberto Houstann, flanked by two guards of his own. They both seemed quite surprised to be seeing each other, and at the same time they turned to Alex and said, "Why is HE still Alive?!"

Alex looked from one to the other, he was not prepared to answer either of them. Roberto turned back to his brother. "It seems you still have terrible taste in assassins, this one betrayed both of us."

Antonio was turning red with rage. "Why are you HERE?"

Alex had to admit he was asking the same question.

Roberto laughed. "Can't a man show up to the unveiling of his brother's new business?" His voice took on a less friendly tone. "I'm here to take it from you."

The two brothers began to circle each other, Antonio pulled a gun out of a boot, And Roberto reciprocated, pulling one out of his suit coat. Antonio spoke. "Reckon we end this once and for all?"

"I could hardly agree more," Roberto responded.

"So how about a duel?" they said together, like a chorus.

Alex wasn't waiting to see who won the duel they both proposed, he was more focused on the brief moment of time that everyone in the room had forgotten him. He carefully pulled a handgun from his own suit coat. His mind was made up, there was only one way to end this now. It may not have been the plan, but when he looked at Jeffrey he knew what he had to do. Alex picked him up with one arm and shot the window. Glass spilled everywhere. Gunshots fired. Alex ran. Leaped. And plummeted towards what remained of the river below. Falling, he clicked the button on the detonator. The dam exploded.

#

Alex pulled himself up wiping hair out of his face, his clothes soaked, his suit coat nowhere to be seen. He turned to the river he had pulled himself out of. The tide had died down to just a rushing river. His eyes followed the stream they connected with the still smoking remains of the dam, and then he remembered, *Jeffrey*. Hurriedly he looked around for his son, hoping he was alive. As he looked he saw a limp form lying in the bank farther down. Running he came to Jeffrey's body, more beaten than Alex's own.

He pulled him from the sand, his strength failed him, he fell to his knees, pulling Jeffrey onto his lap. "Jeffrey, don't die, don't die!" He shook the limp body of his son. "Jeffrey."

As he shook him Jeffrey's eyes began to flutter, he spit sand out of his mouth. "Hey."

Alex could hardly speak, for the first time in years tears leaked out of his eyes, slowly at first as though his face had forgotten how, but soon he was a sobbing wreck.

Jeffrey started to chuckle. "We did it, we actually did it."

Alex smiled through his sobs. "Yes, yes we did." The two sat for a minute. Before Alex helped Jeffrey up, supporting the side of his body with the bullet wound with his arms.

"We did it." he repeated to himself. The two embraced each other in the dying light, father and son, before walking west into the sunset.

Mortal Angels

Nat Jolley

Preface

Out in the universe, there are millions of Creator Gods and Devils that reign over their own Realms of Light and Darkness; the Realm of Light giving a home to all the light angels, and the Realm of Darkness giving a home to all the dark angels. Out of the millions of Creator Gods and Devils, there are two that are significant. Our significant Creator God's name is Exohr, and the Devil is called Dakireth.

What made these two individuals significant was they were the first Creator God and Devil to come to an agreement, but not only that, they decided to create a new realm together for both Light and Dark angels to dwell in. Myths say that their goal was to create harmony, as light and dark angels are opposite of each other, and theologians argue that this was the first discovery of harmony.

Now, in the Realms of Light and Darkness, naturally the angels were just souls living and doing nothing, but the realm that Exohr and Dakireth created was to give the angels real bodies. The realm was then called the Mortal Realm. The Mortal Realm contained lovely and delightful parts, but also dismal and nightmarish parts; and of course, the light and dark angels would stick to what appealed to them the most, for instance, light angels would dwell in the more beautiful places, and for the dark angels, vice versa.

"You never actually meant to kill him! You never wanted to commit that sin!" Araqiel shrieked to herself and looked at her bloody hands and left wrist, the thick, red liquid still dripping from her wrist. Tears were welling up in her eyes, blurring her vision. She held her hand over her wrist to stop the bleeding and turned around, broken glass under her feet, piercing it, letting blood stream out into puddles, but she saw none of it. She was too overwhelmed by her shock, exasperation.

In front of her was a dusty dresser. It creaked from her leaning, palms face down. She didn't care about her cut— any of her cuts —anymore. An open drawer in the dresser caught her eye, and she aggressively slammed it shut.

The bottom half of the mirror frame still held glass, but it was also shattered; it looked like a crooked spider web. Araqiel bent down to see herself in a sliced, tainted reflection. There was her pallid white face, like a decaying pearl. Her straight but tangled dark ebony hair was a dying flower. Her drooping feathered wings, a sad bird on a rainy night. Her bony figure, not much more than a skeleton. Her once gleaming white dress, now blotched cream in some places, scarlet-stained in others. She saw how it hung on her body, like she was a dead tree.

Behind her, something else lay in the distorted reflection. It reminded her of why she was a terrible person, and why she was *originally feeling* terrible. There it lay—the body she had murdered. It was a soulless body now. She hoarsely whispered, "And yet... you didn't—" She swallowed. "You didn't really have much of a choice."

Though he was dead, the body was dark; not pale. It was darker than obsidian. She had killed a dark angel, and now the vivid memory whished back to her consciousness. Araqiel had been gazing out her window, down at the dusty street below. She was fairly high— about five or six stories up, and a fall like that would kill her. And that was her idea. However, she felt that there was a chance that the fall *wouldn't* kill her because she, knowing herself, would get scared and use her wings to save herself, so she turned away and went over to her dresser and opened a drawer. The hollow rolling sound felt loud in the quiet room, especially mixed with her tension; Araqiel felt even more anxiety, and her hands became shaky. Inside the drawer was a dagger— sharp and shiny. She picked it up, and looked at what little reflection there was to see of herself.

With her right hand, she slit open her left wrist.

All of a sudden, Araqiel felt a draft of cold air rush in. She looked up in the mirror, and saw a dark figure swiftly reaching toward her. She gasped as adrenaline blew up in her chest. She whirled around, only to be picked up and thrown at her mirror, leaving it shattered, the top half of glass falling out and jingling down onto the floor. The dagger was flung from Araqiel's hand and somehow ended up on her bed. Grunting, she attempted to get up from the floor, but was shoved down by the dark figure, which passed by her and took the dagger from her bed. In those seconds, Araqiel realized what she was fighting— a dark angel, her opposite. She spread her wings a little and flapped them slightly to help herself up. The dark angel, now facing her again, raised his arm to strike her, but she, despite how short she was and how tall he was, jumped and wrestled the arm that held the dagger, but the dark angel's other arm held Araqiel against his chest, in attempt to prevent her from attacking him, but her legs were free, and she kicked and screamed so hard he had to let her go. She wrangled the dagger from the dark angel, which left some small cuts on her shoulders and neck, but she secured it into her hands, and stabbed the dark angel right into his black, dark heart.

The dark angel gave a great groan, but continued to attack Araqiel, trying to throw her to the ground, but the shove only helped Araqiel yank the dagger right out of the dark angel's chest.

"Where did you even come from?!" Araqiel screamed, forced to back up across the room as the dark angel kept stepping closer to her.

"I was summoned," the dark angel answered. His voice was wavy and deep, and he groaned as she stabbed him again. Deep dark mahogany blood gushed out from his chest and spilled onto the floor. The dark angel stumbled. He fell onto one knee.

Araqiel kicked him all the way down, her need for aggression making her violent. She walked around to the other side of him and watched him take his final breaths.

Araqiel sighed with relief; now she was safe, but the realization of what she had done struck her like a hammer. She looked at her hands, then shrieked. Her eyes widened in horrification. "You never actually meant to kill him! You never wanted to commit that sin!" And then Araqiel brought herself back to the present, and she looked at her hands again.

Araqiel took a deep breath in, and blew it out. She needed to calm down. As she did, she suddenly felt sharp pain; it lanced through her overwhelmed numbness.

It brought her back to herself. Now she noticed the glass shards penetrating into her feet, and the puddles of blood. A breathy, high moan escaped her. She flung herself upon her bed, then tried picking the glass out from her feet. She winced with every pluck and threw each bloody shard down to the floor, not even caring about how she would have to encounter the dangerous clutter of glass later. "How did I not notice this?" She asked herself in her head as tears slowly trickled down her cheeks. Araqiel's feet bled out more with each piece of glass being pulled out and nothing stopping the blood. Araqiel used her bedsheets to wrap her feet in and clot the blood once she was sure all of the glass was out. She let out a sigh of contentment.

She looked at the limp dark body. It was still there, and she wished it were gone, that it had never been. She wailed of agony and shame, and her tears that indicated her physical pain turned to tears of emotional pain, and they flowed down her delicate face. She curled up into a fetal position among the already tangled sheets, trying to find some sort of comfort.

There on her bed, Araqiel sobbed herself to sleep.

There was a large window in Araqiel's room. It let in bright, warm light, but a shadow passed over it, and the air became cold. All was dark except for a small lantern— it was like night had come. It made Araqiel toss and turn in her sleep and give her a disturbing dream. Then she awoke. She sat up with a breathy scream. Sweat wetted Araqiel's forehead, neck, and armpits. Her eyes were wide, like they were petrified, and she trembled like she was freezing.

Even though she knew she was now awake, Araqiel felt as if she were still in her dream, and then she noticed the light in her room had become dim— had she slept that long? The lantern was almost going out. Still in bed, she looked out her window. No sun, no moon, no stars— all darkness. A disturbing feeling hung in the air, and Araqiel felt as if someone had been watching her the whole time she was asleep— then all light went out. She turned her head toward the lantern. "I guess it went out?" she whispered, nearly mouthing the words. At that moment, her paranoia became real. Though the whole room was dark, an even darker shadow stood next to her bedside. Right beside her shoulder. She screamed and snatched her pillow and threw it. It went right through the darkness. A deep sound escaped from whatever was there; it sounded like when you drop a stone in a lake, but without the splash.

"Is something there?!" she screeched. "Who is there?!" Confusion whirled in her mind— what was even there? She was desperate, ready to give in to whatever started torturing her, just to know *what it was.*

The deep sound came again. Then it sounded again, but more laugh-like. Creepy and horrific— Araqiel's mind was overwhelmed with a terrible blackness. She thought it couldn't get any worse, but it did when the being spoke her name.

"Araqiel," the sound deepened when "Araqiel" was spoken.

Chills of terror went down Araqiel's thin spine. "What do you want?!" She shrilled, like a snared bird.

From the darkness, a hand reached out. The voice replied, "You..."

Araqiel gasped. She frantically fumbled to the end of the bed, her legs getting tangled in sheets, trapping her. Araqiel remembered that she had wrapped her feet in the sheets to stop her bleeding. She unwrapped her feet, but the blood had stuck to both the sheets and her skin, and her feet stung as she jerked the cloth away, then presently fell off her bed. Araqiel scrambled to her feet as fast as she could and backed away in the darkness. Her fingers groped through the darkness behind her, searching for the wall, but something cold and lumpy made her trip. She screamed, quick and high, and sidled around, whipping her head back and forth, trying to see what she had tripped over, but could see nothing.

The dark being whirred, murmured.

Araqiel kept backing up. She felt the wall behind her.

The being turned toward her and came closer.

"I want you, Araqiel."

Araqiel began to whimper. "Who are you?" she asked.

Araqiel heard a high, airy whine come from the dark being. Araqiel felt a motion in the air again, like the movement of water against the skin. It brushed toward the dead body. The thing she had tripped over.

"Oh…" Araqiel exhaled, and she glanced in the direction of the window. Araqiel knew she couldn't fight something that wasn't even tangible, unless *it* touched *her*, which was confusing and eerie. Her only option now was to escape. Unfortunately, it was too dark to see. The dead body of the dark angel was lying in front of her; she knew that, and now that she was looking for where the window might be, she felt a draft coming in from there. She only needed to figure out whether the spirit of the dark angel was either to the right or to the left of her. Araqiel hoped that the spirit was to the left because the window was to the right.

Seconds passed, and Araqiel had to make a choice: would she stay put and succumb to the dark spirit, or would she take the chance to escape? What if the spirit *was* between her and the window? "But it shouldn't matter," Araqiel thought, "because the spirit is only able to touch me, and… I can't touch him." With this conclusion, Araqiel leaped over the body in front of her. Her whole body suddenly chilled over— she definitely leapt through the spirit. She stumbled from the sudden cold, and her hands flared out, instinctively trying to catch her fall. Luckily, Araqiel felt the windowsill, and she jumped out. Her hair flew up, and she felt the cold air rush through her dark locks. The air cooled her sweat and tears.

Araqiel blinked her eyes to the sudden evening light of the outdoors. Apparently it wasn't night, and that dark spirit had brought total darkness to her room.

Nearing the ground, Araqiel suddenly panicked, remembering that she actually couldn't fly, despite being an angel and having wings. "Wait!" She gasped, even though her call did nothing. Her arms and legs waved around, and her wings expanded, and to her surprise, she lightly landed on her feet. Her heart beat fast and hard against her chest. She looked up at her bedroom window; it was so high up. It was amazing to her that she had actually jumped from there.

Araqiel looked around at her familiar street. The city was desolate. All of the buildings were the same; tall, shabby, and sepia colored. The cobblestone road was nearly the same color with a tint of gray. The air was dusty, polluted, and hazy. So much that it made it look like the street went on into a beige void forever.

Araqiel turned around to face her building to see if the spirit was following her. She looked up at her window. A dark, shadowy cloud overcame it and swept down the building like a waterfall with an even darker silhouette of a person in the midst of the shadow—the spirit of the dark angel.

"No!" Araqiel gasped and ran up the street as fast as she could. At that moment, she really wished she knew how to fly, but the best she could do to boost her speed was flap her wings as she ran.

The dark angel spirit pursued her, gliding his way over the cobblestones. The dark shadow that accompanied the spirit spread around and over the buildings, and followed the spirit wherever he went. He and his horrific darkness were getting closer and closer.

As Araqiel ran, she noticed that she had started running up a hill— still the street, but it had become steeper. This was making her legs burn and sore, and even her wings were getting tired, but she kept going because she didn't want to know what would happen to her if she gave up.

Gradually, Araqiel was coming to the peak of the hill, and she saw something bright. Araqiel wondered why she had never noticed this light before whenever she actually left her little room, but nonetheless, the light brought Araqiel hope.

Araqiel soon saw that behind the brightness were giant glistening golden gates, and she ran faster. "Are these the Gates of Heaven?" she wondered. Even though Araqiel was a light angel, she wasn't entirely spiritually connected with Exohr. She had always felt lost with herself, and confused about who she really was.

Araqiel reached the Gates, but when she tried opening them and failed, she panicked. She looked behind her, and the dark spirit was closer than she thought. He was just inches away. Araqiel shook the gates, calling for help, but she could see no one.

The darkness and the spirit enveloped her, but she held on tight to the golden bars of the gates. Just when Araqiel thought she was completely doomed and was about to be taken to the Dark Realm of Dakireth, she went right through the closed gates and landed on her hands and knees in a bright, golden, white world.

Araqiel went down on her knees and looked around. She sat on a wide pathway of golden blocks that led through gardens of silver hedges and gold and diamond trees with apples red as rubies, and on the path went until it reached a majestically massive castle made of bright marble with quartz pillars, and all of it was lined with gold finishes. White gold statues of angelic grotesques stood on balconies and beside doorways while triumphantly holding trumpets to their lips. The general architecture of the castle was impeccable and beautifully detailed with details beyond description. Araqiel always believed that Heaven was just a realm with fluffy clouds and apparently felt amazing, but here, there wasn't a cloud to be seen— not even in the sky. The sky was the color of a sapphire, and it glittered the same way.

Araqiel so marveled over the tranquility and quintessence of the world that she didn't notice a man with ivory hair wearing a white robe with golden hemming and a rope of gold tied around his waist.

"Hello there," the man said.

Araqiel shot up in startlement, ready to flee, but once she saw who spoke to her, she stayed and greeted the man.

The man's countenance was pleasant, which was strange to Araqiel. Most men she encountered were hardly amiable or trustworthy. Then the man smiled, and Araqiel felt like it would be wrong to not trust him about anything.

"Welcome to the Realm of Trial," the man said. "I am Ruman, an angel guard here."

Araqiel was immediately confused. "Wait, so this isn't Heaven, and by angel guard, do you mean you're a guardian angel? Shouldn't you be guarding someone?" Araqiel asked skeptically. "This makes sense why I wasn't under any protection. The guardian angels are just slacking." she thought.

Ruman seemed to have read her thoughts. "No, actually, all of the guardian angels are doing their best to protect people. Guard angels are different. We're actually more like guides or companions to those who enter the Realm of Trial."

"Oh," Araqiel said, then repeated her first question. "And is this 'Realm of Trial' not Heaven?"

"No, actually it isn't," Ruman answered. "The Realm of Trial is similar to the Spirit Realm pre-birth, but this is the place where everyone comes to after death—"

"Wait, am I dead?!" Araqiel interrupted, a bit shocked.

"Yes, you were killed by a dark angel," Ruman patiently answered.

"Well that makes sense... I guess," Araqiel said, then she realized that she had interrupted Ruman when he was explaining what the Realm of Trial was, and said, "Oh wait, I'm so sorry; I interrupted you. I didn't mean to do that— I was just a bit surprised that I had died when it didn't even feel like it."

"That's alright," Ruman said kindly. "As I was saying, at the end of the world, on the Day of Judgment, God goes over each light angel's life and makes His judgment to either send the light angel to Heaven or Hell. The same thing actually happens with the dark angels, but their Realm of Trial is a more dark and somber place."

Araqiel felt chills trickle down her spine just at the sound of dark angels.

There was a silence for some moments, then Araqiel said, "I probably won't make it to Heaven…"

"Why ever not?" Ruman asked.

"Well… I… actually, never mind," Araqiel said. She'd rather not admit that she had killed someone, even if it was in self defense.

Ruman slightly tilted his head in a thoughtful way. "Was it pretty bad?" He asked.

Araqiel looked down and swallowed. "Yeah…"

There was another moment of silence, then Ruman said, "I know you don't want to talk about what you did, but if you tell me, I can probably offer you some reassurance…"

Araqiel still didn't look up at Ruman. "I— well…" Tears started welling up in Araqiel's eyes, then she just broke down in sobs, and dropped to her knees. "I–I didn't me—he—he—hean to!" she wailed. "I was ju—just being attacked, and—and I was already really really anx—anxious, and…it just—it just happened!"

Ruman kneeled down in front of Araqiel and took her ice-cold hand. Araqiel looked at Ruman, her crying slowing down a little. Her breath was shaky.

Araqiel swallowed again. "It's just that—" *sniff* "—I was making a bad decision, because I've always felt like a mistake, and..." *Sniff* "...And I wanted to...fix it, but then this dark angel came out of nowhere, and—and—" but Araqiel stopped there and began crying again. "S—sorry..." She whispered.

"It's alright," Ruman whispered back. "I understand now what happened; what you did, and how the dark angel appeared."

Araqiel rubbed her eyes and wiped away her tears and looked back at Ruman. "Really?" She asked. "Please tell me how the dark angel appeared."

"Well," Ruman began, "When someone does something detrimental to themselves, such as attempting suicide, a dark angel is summoned because they love the negative energy and anxiety. They crave it, all the time."

"Oh," was all Araqiel said in response.

There was more silence, this time a bit longer.

Finally, Ruman spoke, saying, "You might just be saved,"

"What?" Araqiel asked.

"You might just be saved," Ruman repeated, then said, "Your guilt and remorse is enough as repentance, and after all, you were defending yourself." He stood up and held out his hand to help Araqiel up to her feet.

"So I will go to Heaven?" Araqiel asked hopefully as she pulled herself up by Ruman's hand.

"Well, it's definitely up to God, but I think there's a chance," The angel said with a smile, and he and Araqiel started walking down the golden pathway.

"I'm Araqiel, by the way," Araqiel said.

"Nice to meet you, Araqiel," Ruman said, and they disappeared into the gardens.

The Chance of Another Lifetime

Jesstyn Campbell

Deep in the folds of time, a woman stirred. No sound, no person had awoken her—just a feeling in the air.

Someone needed her.

The woman arose, throwing her cloak over her shoulders. She paused, feeling the air. She needed to know how many there were.

Two. As usual.

She took two vials from her infinite collection and stowed them in her cloak.

Without another word, she ventured out into the universe. Moments later, she had arrived.

Hidden in the shadows near the tomb, the woman watched the two families grieve over the bodies of their dead children. Others stood by, arguing, trying to determine what must have happened.

As though it wasn't obvious, thought the woman.

A boy had loved a girl. The girl had loved him back. When each was faced with the idea of a life without the other, both chose death. In the most tragic of ironies, they had died beside each other.

Such was the course of forbidden love.

For centuries, their story would be told. Before long, everyone would assume it was fiction. But, for now, it was still very, very real.

Patiently, the woman waited for the people to disperse. Though she didn't share it, she understood their grief. It was no small thing to lose a child; an even larger thing to lose one to an enemy. Once, she would have wished to comfort them, to reveal herself and her purpose—but the centuries had taught her that it was better if they didn't know. It was not the way of things.

Long past midnight, the crowd slowly left the tomb, leaving an eerie silence in their wake. It seemed that even the creatures of the night dared not penetrate the darkness with their cries.

It was time.

Quietly, she crept to the entrance and surveyed the scene before her. There were the lovers; barely more than children, the woman thought. And a third—what was he doing here?

No matter. He was not her ward.

She was here for the lovers, who had delivered themselves to her the moment that flask had met lips, blade had met breast. *They* were her ward, and them she would redeem.

Their spirits had lingered; she could feel them. Banished from their bodies, but present still. Waiting.

The woman removed the two vials from her cloak.

"Come," she whispered.

Eagerly, they came to her. Alive, they had not known her, but in death they knew she was their only hope. They knew, like the earth knows the sun will rise. They knew, like a baby knows to cry. Though the vials were a temporary prison, it was their way to freedom. They settled within.

"One day," she whispered; a promise to the dead.

And then she was gone.

~*~

Neon lights and resounding bass greeted Jen like a long-awaited friend as she stepped through the double doors into the wonderful chaos of high school prom. A grin spread over her face as she took it all in; the balloons, the streamers, the flashy photo booth. A giant banner on one wall read "Pine Creek High School, 2023."

Beside her, Sophie breathed deeply, her eyes beginning to sparkle. Jen laughed. She knew there was no place her eccentric, high-energy best friend would rather be.

"Oh, *yes*," said Sophie, grabbing Jen's hand and dragging her into the dance.

Jen poked her.

"So," she said. "Where is he?"

A shy smile spread across Sophie's face, her eyes scanning the room as she chewed her lip. Suddenly, her hand tightened around Jen's.

"Right there," she said, pointing. "Red hair. Purple tie."

Jen peered through the crowd and picked out a small group standing beside the drink table, her eyes landing on a young man among them.

Jen's breath caught. She knew that face. That brown hair, the way it curled slightly—and that smile. She knew that smile.

The more she studied him, she became less certain that she had ever seen him before—and yet, more certain that she knew him somehow.

"Look at his face," said Sophie. "He looks like she's driving him crazy."

Jen barely heard her.

"Yeah," she said faintly. "What?" She realized Sophie was looking at the guy beside the mystery boy, a tall redhead who currently had a girl in a shimmering pink dress hanging from his arm. "Oh—yeah. Yeah, he totally does. Her dress clashes with his hair, too."

Sophie giggled.

"Look at his friend," said Jen. "Does he look familiar to you?"

Sophie peered through the crowd, cocking her head as she studied him.

"No," she said. "I don't think I've ever seen him before."

Sophie knew practically everyone in the school. If anyone would know him, she would.

Jen looked back at him, intrigued.

He glanced around the room. Their eyes met.

An unexpected jolt of pain seared through Jen's chest. She gasped, pressing a hand to her heart.

"Jen?" asked Sophie, sounding concerned. "Are you okay?"

Jen took a deep breath, then nodded. The pain had gone as quickly as it had come.

"Yeah," she said after a moment. "I just felt a weird pain, but it's gone now. I'm fine."

"Hm." Sophie looked at her thoughtfully, then seemed to decide to trust her. Her eyes sparkled. "Well, as long as you're not having a heart attack, wanna go get drinks?"

~*~

Ryan glanced around the room, taking in the sights as he laughed at Kendall's latest joke. Out of a spontaneous burst of friendliness—or pity, one of the two—the girl next door had invited him to prom. Having just moved into the area, Ryan had expected that visiting a school that wasn't his would be awkward, but this... this was fun.

Ryan paused. That girl, standing by the punch bowl... where had he seen her before?

As the others continued talking, he nudged Hailey.

"Who is that?" he asked quietly. "In the silver dress."

"That's Jen," said Hailey. "I'm graduating with her next week. She's super fun. Why?"

"No reason," said Ryan. "She just...looks kind of familiar."

"Hm," said Hailey. "Aren't you from Arizona?"

"Yup." Ryan nodded. "There's no way I've seen her before, but...I guess she just reminds me of someone." He wasn't sure who, though.

His attention was broken as a young man approached them.

"Look at you," he said with a sly smile, nudging Kendall. "I didn't know you were dating anyone."

Kendall's face turned a color that clashed violently with his hair.

"Oh, we're not dating," he said quickly. "We just...came to prom together."

Lily, Kendall's date, looked mildly put out.

"Ah," said the newcomer. "In that case, may I steal her for a dance?"

Ryan hadn't noticed the music change. The beginnings of a slow song were now playing over the loudspeakers and couples were already gathering in the middle of the room.

"Sure," said Kendall. Based on what he had observed for the past several minutes, Ryan thought he did a very good job at not sounding eager to get rid of her.

Lily, beaming once again, allowed herself to be whisked away onto the dance floor.

"Thank goodness," Kendall said under his breath. "There's a girl I really want to ask... but I wasn't sure *she'd* be okay with it." He gestured to Lily, who was giggling girlishly at something her partner had just said. He cocked a smile, clapping Ryan on the shoulder. "Come help me out, will you? She's had another girl stuck to her all night." He winked.

Ryan looked to Hailey, who nodded encouragingly.

"You're supposed to be meeting more people," she said. "So go do that."

It didn't take long for Ryan to realize that Kendall was making a beeline for the weirdly familiar girl and her friend.

~*~

Sophie grabbed Jen's arm, nearly making her spill fruit punch on herself.

"Watch it!" said Jen.

Sophie ignored her. "Is it just me, or is he coming over here?" she said, her voice higher than usual.

Jen looked in the direction Sophie was staring and froze. Kendall *was* moving their way—and he wasn't alone.

"Don't stare," she said, taking another sip of punch. "He might not be coming to us." *They* might not.

Most likely, they weren't. There were countless girls in this general direction; it was silly to assume it was for them. They would be asking girls they knew, right? Sophie had barely known Kendall for a week, and his friend had no idea who Jen was... and it was probably just an accident that he was making eye contact with her again, and coming closer...

~*~

"Would you like to dance?" Ryan asked. Up close, the girl's eyes were brown, with flecks of gold—the way Ryan had known they would be. Somehow.

"I'd love to," she said with a smile. It struck Ryan like a lightning bolt. He had seen that smile before, though the memory eluded him. Some part of him knew... he loved that smile.

Ryan offered his hand and she took it, allowing him to lead her onto the dance floor. Even her touch felt familiar. He spun her around and took her waist, beginning to move to the music.

"I'm Ryan," he said. "Have we met? You look kinda familiar."

"Jen," she said. "Funny—I was thinking the same thing about you."

THE END

The Ballad of George

Garrison Bird

George was your average Costco shopper. He was also your average Cyborg. His only programming was to love shopping at Costco. He went seven times a day with money supplied by the government. The government benefited from this by getting free samples (even though they are already free).

One day during his fifth routine visit that day, George noticed that a man in a hood had a Costco card pop out of his wrist. He searched his database to see if this was regular human behavior. Based on that knowledge, he decided it was something unusual. George decided that he would follow the hooded stranger. As George was following him, he noticed other non-human signs, like his skin would become metal for a second then flash back to normal skin . He decided to throw food at the hoodie man to see if it would go through him or not. He threw the sample that he was eating, which was hard for George because he loved samples. The man hadn't seemed to notice he had been pelted with food.

George was confused so he kept following. Next the hooded man put 3 barrels of motor oil in his cart, and this really confused George. He thought, why is he buying 3 barrels of motor oil? Then a portable battery went into the man's cart.

Suddenly everything started to make sense. George gathered all the courage from his database and moved forward to confront him. He chose a deep and intimidating voice from his audio file and commanded. "Hey you! Off with your hood!"

The startled stranger started to run away so George chased him down the food aisle and corralled him in the dairy section. This frightened George to death because his mom told him he was lactose intolerant, but he worked up the courage to tackle the man. They both fell into a crate of cottage cheese which spilled into George's eyes and mouth and he realized that cottage cheese was amazing.

He started sucking up the cottage cheese because the hooded man was buried in it. Every slurp brought him closer and closer, until at last he looked up to find the hood was gone. What? Was this a mirror? George felt he was looking at himself....but instead, it was another cyborg. Just as George was about to pull out the stranger's motherboard wallet to identify who he was, a deep voice whispered...something...but he never got to hear

And as everything faded to black, background music swelled up.

When he woke he found himself in an outhouse that smelled like old stale fish. It looked like someone had taken brown, green, and red paint and squirted it all over the walls, and the roof. When he touched it to make sure it was safe to bang on the walls. It felt squishy, crusty, moldy, dry, and wet all at the same time. When he touched it, it burst all over George covering him in a reddish greenish goop.

Then he tried the door which was locked. He was trapped. Then the smell wafted up his nostrils. The smell was so bad he could taste it and it was as if he was licking a hairy maggot-infested dog corpse.

It looked like No one had ever bothered to clean it. it was so dirty and smelled so bad whoever tried to clean it would need a hazmat suit. But those are expensive and what janitor has that kind of money? It was at that point that it hit him. He had an emergency hazmat suit in his chest cavity.

So he whipped it out and put it on. He thought to himself if I am locked in and can't get out then I want to spend time here in a clean space. So he started scrubbing. It took him all day and night. When he finished he sat on the toilet and suddenly the door swung open.

Then he was blasted with the light from the midday sun. When he walked out he found a mysterious figure at the back of McDonalds. George approached the mysterious figure. The figure spun around and saw George approaching. "What are you doing here?" he said.

George said, "I was at Costco chasing another Cyborg when I was transported to that outhouse over there. It was so dirty that I had to put on my emergency hazmat suit on so I could clean it. What are you doing here?"

"I came here to find the legendary Pizza Hut box that is fabled to be behind this very McDonalds and is the only thing that can vanquish Lida the Sorcerer."

"Well then I will help you," George said.

They were off. They continued down the alleyway until they found a brown fluffy statue of Lida the Sorcerer.

At first they were afraid. When people found statues of Lida they usually disappeared. but this one was different from the usual. All the other statues were not brown and fluffy, but gold and shiny. At closer inspection, this statue was actually Mida, Lida's twin sister.

She also had a note in her hand that said "Ye who come looking for a Pizza Hut box must pass two trials. The first of which is you must go into McDonalds and order the 100 Chicken McNuggets box and eat it all gone. Then you must bring the box to the brown fluffy statue of Mida and burn it at her feet and the ashes will tell you what to do next."

"Then that is exactly what we will do," George said. They walked to the front of the McDonalds and ordered the 100

Chicken McNuggets box and it was so big that they both had to carry it to the table.

When it was on the table George took the first bite. He chewed for a few seconds and suddenly there was a loud crunch. He immediately spit it out. They were both nervous to eat any more.

So George thought of a plan. "I will go to the store across the street and buy a blender so we can blend them all into a paste then we can cook them again." When George came back they put them in a blender and blended them up.

When they were done they asked a worker if they could use one of the fryers. The worker said yes on account of them giving him a twenty dollar tip. They started frying them and in thirty minutes they were done and could finally eat the Chicken Mcnuggets.

They started getting fat as they started eating the Chicken McNuggets. When they were done they looked like bloated cows. When they got up to leave they were so fat they knocked over tables and caused havoc and were kicked out of McDonalds and were not allowed to return. They waddled to the back and found the statue of Mida and burned the Chicken McNugget box. When it was all burned up the wind picked up and blew the ashes into this message. "You must travel to Paris and find a giant turkey."

~~~

Zach lived in a sewer in Paris. One day he overheard some people talking about how they were sending in crews to clean the sewer! That is terrible, he thought. He would surely be found and they would make him take a bath.

He was very scared of being clean. Being clean meant no maggots in his beard for midnight snacks. It meant he wouldn't smell like his favorite dung. Yes, taking a bath would be awful so he hatched a plan. He decided to dress up as a turkey but there was one flaw in his plan: it was November.

So when he heard someone coming he dressed up and confronted the person. They were so frightened they took a picture and ran as fast as they could.

He thought his troubles were over but they had just begun. When the person got back home he posted it online. It went all over the news and everyone all over the country wanted that turkey for their thanksgiving dinner.

All the hunters from all over the countryside went hunting for the mysterious giant turkey.

~~~

George suddenly got a notification that a giant turkey had been spotted in the sewers in Paris. "A giant turkey has been spotted in the sewers in Paris," George said.

"Well what are we waiting for? Let's go," the mysterious person said. They called a taxi and left to go to the airport.

When they got on the airplane George asked the mysterious man, "What is your name?"

"My name is Pablo Señor Rodriguez Jr."

"Why are you trying to get the Pizza Hut box?"

"I am trying to get it because the evil sorcerer Lydia kidnapped my family and the only way to get them back is to kill her with the Pizza Hut box."

When they landed they got off and immediately headed to go find Pablo's friend Diablo leAmondWater because he worked in the sewer. They were hoping he would help them get into the sewer to find the giant turkey.

Pablo's friend agreed to help them find the giant turkey. When they got to the sewer, George scanned the area for a giant turkey. His excellent scanners found it right away.

George also found something else–there was a hunter laying in wait with a gun ready to shoot it for Thanksgiving dinner.

When George told everyone, Pablo said, "We need to help. It is the only way to get my family back. Let's go." He ran off the way George had pointed.

"Wait!" George said, "I was just stretching my finger. It is the opposite way." With that Pablo stopped and ran the other way with the rest of the gang on his tail.

When they got to the turkey it was cowering in a corner telling the hunter to not shoot. "That is weird," George thought to himself. "Even in France the turkeys speak English."

Then he came to his senses. This was a person in a turkey costume. He had to save the figure because he or she was the key to finding the Pizza Hut box. (George didn't know the gender of the turkey being.)

George ran up to the hunter and grabbed his gun and shoved it down his throat and then threw him into the slow moving sludge.

Pablo ran up to the turkey and ripped its mask off and said, "Where is the Pizza Hut box!"

"I don't know what you are talking about," he said.

"TAKE US TO THE PIZZA HUT BOX!"

"Ok, ok I will take you to where I live. I don't know if there is a Pizza Hut box there but we can look." When they got to their destination a terrible smell wafted up their noses and they all vomited. The turkey person laughed and walked over to a pile of poop and smothered himself with it. When everyone recovered from the smell they started searching for the Pizza Hut box. After 5 hours they finally found it. When they opened it a giant laser beamed out of it. They quickly closed the box.

"That will do," Pablo said. Next they needed to find where Lida's evil lair was. "How will we find it if no one has ever found it?"

"Let's look all over the Pizza Hut box and see if there are any clues," George said.

When they looked on the bottom of the box they found a map that led to Lida's evil lair. It was located in a country named Azerbaijan.

"Where is this strange country?" Pablo asked George.

"It is in Asia and touches Russia, Georgia, Armenia, and Iran."

"Wait, I thot Georgia was a state in America."

George projected a map onto the wall. A chorus of ooohhhhhhs rang up from everyone as they realized where it was. "We better get going. It is 2276 miles away."

~~~

4 Days Later

~~~

When they got to the x on the map they arrived in a small Azerbaijani village called Qasımkənd that was surrounded by barren wasteland.

They saw an abandoned warehouse at the end of the main dirt road. That looked like a good place to investigate. While they were investigating they observed that there was no door but there was a greeting mat at a random spot by a wall.

"What do you think this is for?" Pablo said. Suddenly he tripped and tumbled into the wall where the mat was and rolled through the wall. He walked back through the wall and said, "Found the entrance."

"I have a plan to defeat Lida," George said. "You guys stay here." Then George ran into the building with the pizza box. When he was in he disguised himself as a pizza delivery guy and went up to Lida and said, "Your pizza is here."

Lida said, "I didn't order pizza."

George opened the Pizza Hut box aimed straight at her head and bbbbbeeeeeeezzzzzzzzzzzzz her head exploded and her lifeless body fell to the ground. The Pizza Hut box disintegrated into ashes.

Outside, Pablo suddenly got a phone call from his wife. When he finished the phone call, George walked out of the building. George said, "Our work is done."

~~~

1 Day Later

~~~

They got out of the airport and waited there for the Buick Roadmaster station wagon that Pablo's wife owned. When it rolled up out came 6 children and Pablo's wife. After a few minutes they got into the car and rode into the sunset.

The End

Connect the Dots

Anna Miles

Chapter One

For the third time this morning, the blaring wakeup call tore through the silence of the morning, demanding that my embrace with sleep be disrupted. I searched for the *snooze* button on my alarm, my head still in my pillow. I already knew that today hated me. And likewise, I hated today. Especially since today was the start of the last school week before spring break.

"You better not press snooze again, young man."

I groaned, "Mom, I need my sleep." My voice was muffled from my pillow.

"Funny. Get up, Nikko."

"Fine."

A moment later I faintly heard her footsteps move into the hall, probably going to go get my twin, Cilisia, to wake her up as well. I rolled onto my back, the rays of the morning sun streaming into my room. I looked over to my gray nightstand, the photo of my dad, my sister, and me still there, like it had been my entire life. It was a lot more significant for me than it used to be, my dad had died three years ago.

In the photo my dad held me and my sister as babies in front of our Christmas tree. His expression was gleeful and so familiar. I still didn't know if I should be happy that I got to have him for 14 years, or sad that he was gone. He was going on a work trip and his plane went down, I hadn't been the same since. I noticed that the simple copper colored frame surrounding the memory was getting kind of dusty. I'd deal with that later. I looked at my watch, *7:25am.*

I got out of bed and dragged myself to my insane assortment of polo shirts. Private school problems. I nearly face planted on my way over, I *really* needed to clean my room. I added that to my mental list of things to do. I picked a burgundy polo and some khakis. After changing I threw some gel in my curls, admiring myself in the bathroom mirror. I was a disheveled mess, and the ladies loved it. The burgundy complimented my curly chestnut hair and fair skin. My eyes were interesting because one was ice blue, and one was half blue, half golden brown. Attractiveness "problems." I finished my morning routine and exited my bed chamber. I got approximately two steps down the hall before I heard a huff of anger.

"Ugh, do you perfectly time leaving your room at the same time as me?" My twin, Cilisia, was clearly excited to see me. "I'll have you know, I am not in the mood for whatever shenanigans you have planned."

Women.

"You're lame. Ladies first, I guess," I gestured for her to go down the stairs. She lifted her hand into a loose fist, her middle and pointer finger hovering in front of her ice blue eyes, she then pointed them at me, in a classic "I've got my eyes on you" look, I put my hands up defensively. She flipped her long brown curls and started down the stairs.

In the spacious living room my mom was sitting on the white sectional, flipping through T.V. stations, "Took you people long enough," Mom said. I looked at my watch.

"It's only 7:40, we have plenty of time."

"Yeah, but I made a good breakfast. It's on the counter."

"Sweet!" I walked through the living room arch to the kitchen. There were waffles, eggs, hashbrowns and bacon on the counter. Along with a bunch of toppings.

My sister walked in behind me, looking rather smug now as she dished up her food, "You remembered to practice for our French quiz today, right?"

I froze. That's what it was that I had forgotten, I knew there was something else I needed to do, and this was what it was. I was gonna fail. I had all A's, which meant my French grade wasn't crying *and* crashing *and* burning. Yet. What kind of Ivy League takes someone who fails a French quiz? How do you say "I'm screwed" in French? Because that was what I was: screwed. I guess this is what you get when you only make lists in your head and not on paper.

"Of course I remembered. What kind of idiot forgets to practice their French." THIS IDIOT DID! You can call me Captain Failure now.

#

"Soooooooo, you're totally in love with me. That's what I'm getting out of this conversation."

"Uh, absolutely not, just because I argue with you, doesn't mean I'm 'in love' with you! Do you even have a brain?"

Raeja liked it, I know she did. "Who needs a brain when ya got love?"

"I. Am. Not. In. Love. With. You."

"Oh really? Most ladies would totally wish they had a chance with me but noooooooo, you have to make my life harder by trying to break my ego."

"Yes, yes I do, you can't just flirt with a girl and always expect her to be in love with you, that's idiotic." Her gentle voice didn't sound so gentle anymore.

"Only idiotic for you, amour." I was getting good at this.

"I just threw up in my mouth."

"Hey, I wasn't doing that bad! You liked it, admit it."

"No, I'm not admitting something that is against everything I believe in!"

"You're so cute when you get mad."

"Ugh… you little piece of shi—"

I cut her off. "Woahhhhh girly, chill with the lingo."

She pursed her lips, seeming to be trying not to smile. "Bye, Nikko, I'm done here."

"Yeah, okay, whatever."

I was in the school hallway near my French class, 'arguing' with one of the hottest girls in school, Raeja Valentine. Most girls fell all over me, but the only one I had interest in was Raeja. I mean, I'd say I knew her pretty well too, she was my twin sister's best friend, so she came by a lot. I watched her as she left.

"You've seriously got to stop doing that." Apparently Cilisia had heard the whole thing go down.

"I'm just following what my heart desires. That is a bit awkward that you were stalking me though."

"I'm not stalking you, I have French next period too. It's kind of hard to miss either way. You guys are always arguing, you're kind of loud, and just about everyone notices you."

The bell rang.

"She'll come through some day."

"Gross."

"After you, your royal sisternance."

We walked into the classroom and took our seats. I hoped my teacher would forget we had a term final. Of course, my sister immediately turned and asked if her friend was ready for the quiz, and said, "I'm super excited! I studied a ton and am practically fluent by now." I was sure she intentionally said that loudly to rub it in my face. She wasn't fluent, but she was doing better than me.

"We will take the quiz to start. I hope you are all prepared, it makes up a good portion of your term grade. Good luck." Mr. Baugh started passing out the papers. When it got to me, I looked at the page and had no idea how this would go. I did remember how to write my introduction at least. Goodbye all A's, we had a good run.

\#

"Mother dearest, we're home!" I called across the house.

My mom walked in, her purse in hand. "Perfect. I'm going to the store, any requests?"

"Goldfish, and those weird pickle chips," I said.

Cilisia chimed in. "Oooooo, get some of those spicy Dorito things."

"Okay, I'll be back in an hour."

"Bye."

As I suspected, today did hate me. Unsurprisingly, I failed the French quiz. This brought my grade down to a C+ overall. That hurt, like really bad. And to add to my state of distress, in P.E. I got nailed in the shoulder with a baseball because my friend, Luke, sucks at pitching. I went to the kitchen and got a snack and put some ice in a Ziplock bag for my shoulder, then I went upstairs and threw my backpack on my bed, followed by myself. I pulled out my phone and started scrolling on Instagram, holding the ice to the sore spot.

There were a lot of random videos, but one caught my attention. Some reporter lady was talking about the government system. Some people who married illegally had disappeared. I put the ice down on the nightstand.

Three years ago, the government started a system to bring down the number of divorces. Everyone got a different colored dot on the inside of their wrist when they turned 17, and the goal was to marry someone who had a dot of the same, or similar color. The closer the color, the higher the compatibility. It was a really stupid prospect, why did they think they got to choose who we got to love. So much for, "The government only wants the best for you." Were they psychopaths?

I turned 17 in less than a week, on Friday. Not gonna lie, I had pretty much forgotten about that…

Raeja's dot was a lilac purple. I hoped mine was the same. I'm not a huge fan of purple, but I am a huge fan of Raeja, so it overcompensates.

I lay there staring at the ceiling.

What would I do if I had some completely different color?

Chapter Two

The rest of last week went something like this: going to school, annoying my sister, and trying to *not* annoy Raeja. I had a bit of a change of heart and now wanted her to enjoy my existence, either as friends or as *more* than friends. I found out a few interesting things about her when she came over to hang out with Cilisia every single day. I had been really trying to make her think I was a decent human being behind my good looks. I was actually kind of getting somewhere with her now.

I found out that Raeja was an intern for the government administration. And we know how much I just love the system. She brought up her older sister and how she was trying to find a way to not get caught falling in love with a polar opposite color. I asked her why she told me that, because it seemed pretty secretive. She told me, "I needed to tell someone, it's driving me crazy. I trust you. Don't make me regret it." That was comforting... Just kidding. My sister pulled her away soon after.

On Thursday, I was sitting on the living room couch, doing my French homework when I heard the front door open. I turned to find Cilisia and Raeja walking in the house. They were laughing about something.

"I'm gonna go get my stuff, I'll be right back," Cilisia said. She went upstairs.

After my sister was hopefully out of earshot I asked Raeja, "What are you ladies up to today?"

She must not have noticed me when they walked in because she jumped. "Oh, uh, we're going to the mall and stuff. I would invite you but Lis would be pretty mad at me if I did that."

She was right, my lovely sister wouldn't have approved of that.

"That's okay, I'm hanging out with Alec soon."

"That sounds fun." She looked down at her feet, hesitating before she asked, "So, what are you doing this weekend?"

"The day has finally come," I said.

Raeja gave an adorable eye roll and met my gaze. "Get over yourself, you're still pretty annoying. But I like it. I also liked how you were before you tried to be socially acceptable."

"I knew it!!"

She tucked a strand of perfect blonde hair behind her ear. "I take that as you do want to do something?"

"I mean my birthday is tomorrow but I can do something on Saturday if you want."

"Saturday works. I'll let you know what the plan is."

I heard footsteps coming down the stairs. I gave Raeja a wink, she blushed. I went back to my work. Trying to hide my own face.

"Okay, I've got everything, let's go Ra—" Cilisia cut herself off. I could practically feel her turn to stare daggers at the back of my head. "Why does your face look like that Rae?"

"Let's just go, please," Raeja suggested.

"You're going to have to tell me at some point, I hope you know."

"Fair enough."

I heard the door open and close again. I was pretty much exploding at this point. Raeja had really just asked me out, or maybe she just wanted to hangout but I didn't care. This was the moment I had been waiting for for the past two years.

At about eight that night I got a message from Raeja. My phone screen lit up and, unfortunately, Alec noticed it before I got to it.

He picked it up. "OoooOOoooOooOo, Nikko!! It's Raeja!"

"Give me that."

He turned away, keeping my phone from me and he opened it. I shouldn't have told him my password. I think he had started reading the message before I practically tackled him.

"Alright alright, take it." He handed it to me and I put it in my back pocket. "Are you guys dating now or something?" He asked.

"No…"

"Really? She seemed like she was talking about something like that."

"Shut up."

"Whatever man. I gotta go, I have to do my history homework and stuff."

I walked him to the door.

After I closed the door behind him I immediately pulled out my phone. I was so ready for this conversation.

> Raeja: *I'm still really hoping to hangout or whatever we're gonna call it on Saturday. I do have a party thing for my internship though. So a work party kind of. I forgot I had already told them I'd go, so you should come.*
>
> Me: *I'm cool with that. What time?*
>
> Raeja: *Around 6, we prolly wanna leave at like 5:45 tho*
>
> Me: *Do you want me to pick you up?*
>
> Raeja: *Sure*

Me: *Okay great, see you there*

This was actually happening! How was I supposed to get out of the house without my sister finding out where I was going though... That was going to be tough, because she pretty much always knows when I'm hiding something. I guess I'd worry about it when it came.

Chapter Three

My birthday was actually eventful, to my surprise. Cilisia had actually made plans for herself. She had about 40 people over for *her* party and my mom threw me in so it was a combined celebration. Why did we have to share a birthday? It was weird because I didn't know most of the people. It was very last second, but Alec and a few other of my other friends did show up.

I was actually having fun. We had a ton of snacks and we had a campfire so we made smores and we had a movie playing on the projector screen on our back porch, everyone just did their own thing. Raeja was at the party, but we hadn't said much, she was acting pretty shy. After a long while of convincing myself to say something to her, I found her at our soda/ snack bar.

"Hey, Rae," I said, mimicking my twin sister's voice.

"Hi, Nikko," She said. Her voice was even softer than usual, but the look in her eyes was anything but soft.

"I see you are quite the anti-social right now."

She pretended to be surprised, "Weird, I had no idea."

"Ha. Ha. You are so funny."

"Thanks, I try." She seemed annoyed.

"Golllyyyyyy, tone down the fire eyes, will ya?"

She shook her head. "Sorry, I'm just not really myself right now."

"Yeah, I kind of noticed that. Not in a stalker way though. I promise. Forget I said that actually... Want to tell me what's wrong?"

"No, not really. Maybe some other time. I think I'm going to go though. Hopefully I'll be in a better mood for our outing tomorrow if I get good sleep."

I had no idea what to say, so I just let her walk away. She was probably going to find my sister.

Maybe a minute later, Alec and my friend Bryce walked up to me.

I was sure they both saw straight through my fake smile. "Somebody is looking a bit down," Alec said.

"For real. Did you get the wrong color of dot or something?" Bryce asked.

I had totally forgotten about that. "I actually haven't checked." I put my hand on the right-side sleeve of my white hoodie. That was usually the side it was on. Bryce and Alec both waited in anticipation. "3... 2... 1..." I pulled the sleeve back. There was nothing there. I checked the other wrist. Still nothing.

"I guess it hasn't kicked in yet. Bummer."

"It took me like, two days." Alec said.

"Yeah, it took a week for my sister's dot to come in," Bryce said.

Suddenly Alec started laughing. "Wait, Bryce, what if Lindsey had the same dot as Nikko?! Man, that would be crazy," He started fanning himself with his hand. "She's smoking hot too."

Bryce did not like that prospect. "Ew, don't ship Nikko and my sister. She's married."

"I didn't get a chance with her, so hopefully Nikko will. Besides, a guy wants what a guy wants."

"Gee am I glad that the guys don't get to choose."

"Technically no one does."

I wasn't paying attention to the conversation at hand. I was just worried about Raeja, and what shade of the colorful splotch I would get. The rest of the night was a blur.

When I woke up the next morning, I immediately checked for my dot. Nothing. When I was in the shower I checked. Also nothing. It was the same for when I checked three times during breakfast. Cilisia was still asleep, but my mom must've noticed my stress from my lack of food consumption. She slid me a plate of fruit.

"Honey, eat something. Your dot is not that big of a deal, you don't need to worry so much. I am positive that some perfect girl will be in your color range."

"I know, I'm just nervous for my date tonight. She was acting weird yesterday and wouldn't tell me what was up."

"I mean, she isn't just going to tell you everything right after you become a sixteenth of the scale of friendship closer."

"That made no sense."

"You are correct, sometimes I even confuse myself."

I smiled.

#

Raeja and I were about twenty minutes into our date and it was going pretty well. I really wanted to address what was up yesterday though. So I asked her. "This is kind of random, but I actually have a question. Why were you acting so off yesterday?"

"I had a feeling you would ask that, and I'm not really sure why, I was probably just tired or-" She was cut off by her phone dinging. Everyone in the room turned to look at her, she quickly pulled it out to silence it. Her face turned a bit red.

"I probably should've thought of that earlier." She was scanning her phone, seeming to be reading a message. She looked up at me, I couldn't read her expression, it had most definitely changed from embarrassment though. She adjusted her stance. "You're the only one I told." She pointed an accusing finger at me. "Did you turn her in?"

I smacked her hand down and asked, "What? Turn who in?" I was confused beyond belief.

"My sister. It was you, you told."

"I did not tell anyone anything, especially not about that." A lot of people were watching us, and I doubted she wanted other people to know. "Can we talk about this somewhere else? Everyone is staring at us."

She did not take that well. "My sister just got taken by the government and could quite literally be dead, and you're worried about how this conversation looks?!"

"Yes, I am worried about it." I grabbed her arm and dragged her out, she fell silent. She did struggle a bit but I continued to drag her through the hall and out the door of the building. The sun was starting to set when we got outside. I finally dropped her arm. She bit her lips and looked away.

"I swear on my dead father's life it wasn't me. Plus, I don't even care that your sister chose that for herself. If anything, kudos to her. The system is a ridiculous method of achieving anything anyways."

She still hadn't looked at me, there were a few beats of silence before I heard an inhale. "Will you just take me home? Please."

"Sure, after you tell me why you think I would do that." The moment the words left my mouth I wish I could've taken them back. "Sorry, I didn't mean to sound like that."

Her tone was cold. "Do you seriously think you're above sounding like that? I hate to break it to you, but you *are* the type to do that. And apparently the type to be a narc. What a pity. Can we go now?"

"Yeah." I was heartbroken.

I drove her home in silence. A very awkward silence. I tried not to be too obvious when I looked over at her. I was really annoyed that she thought I'd do that, but what if she was right that I was just some silly guy? I didn't want to say anything further.

I noticed there was a black Toyota Tacoma already parked in her driveway, so I pulled in on the opposite side of it. "Well, this is your stop." I put the blue 2017 Honda Civic in park and got out of the car. She still hadn't said a word. I imagined she had plenty of profanities ricocheting off of the sides of her brain though.

As one does, I walked around to the passenger side door and opened it, I offered my hand to her. She ignored it. Absolutely brutal. "Thanks for the ride," she said bitterly. And she walked into the house.

"Geez," I whispered to myself, shaking my head. I was lifting my hands to my steering wheel to pull out of the driveway, and that is when I noticed the *lilac purple* dot on the inside of my right wrist. Maybe a few shades darker than Raeja's, but definitely within the same range. We were compatible.

That color seemed like a curse now.

I sat in the car, reflecting on what all was happening. After a while I realized I probably seemed creepy, so I pulled away. I mindlessly drove home. I didn't know how to describe how I was feeling at this point, I thought it was mostly that I was bothered by how quick she was to blame me. Maybe she wasn't who I thought she was... She never stood out to me as the type to play the blame game.

Love is blind.

Chapter Four

I pulled out my phone to see if I had any missed messages or calls. "She hasn't answered my texts or calls, I dunno what to do at this point." I set my phone down. I was now three days into spring break, it was Wednesday. We were at Chick-Fil-a and I was talking to Alec about Raeja. After our date I decided I was going to check on her and tell her about my dot, even though it probably wouldn't have done anything. Even if it was going to change something, she hadn't been responding.

"She's probably just with her family, I mean, her sister is gone to who knows where. She could very likely be on a trip too. It is a break after all." He licked his ice cream cone. "Have you asked Cilisia?"

"Heck no, I am not about to tell her that her best friend hates me now. And especially not telling her I took her best friend out."

"Well, I dunno what to tell you, dude."

"Yeah, I didn't really expect you to. I guess I'll just wait till after break. Maybe she'll show up at my house to hang out with Cilisia."

"Glad we dealt with that. Now, let's finish our food and go find some hot chicks. That worker over there seems like a good start for me." He pointed to a girl with strawberry blonde hair and an emerald-green mark. Alec's was teal, but at least they were in a similar color category.

I rolled my eyes. "You are such a weirdo."

Alec ended up chickening out and didn't end up talking to the worker.

We were leaving the restaurant when a girl walked up to me, seeming to have left her friend.

"Hey, I'm Tuscany."

I blinked a few times. "Uh, hey."

"Sorry, this is super random," She leaned in, lowering her tone. "My friend dared me to come ask for your number."

I glanced back at the other girl. "Right, but is that really the only reason?"

She blushed. "Yes, obviously. Can I have it or not?"

"Sure. Why not? You have a pretty name by the way." She handed me her phone and I typed in my contact information.

"Thanks."

I cracked a smile. "Of course. I'm Nikko by the way." I gave her phone back.

"Thank you." She slipped the device into her back pocket, she had a plum dot. "I'll text you." She walked away.

"That was wild. You are such a ladies man," Alec said.

"No one has done something like this for so long. Besides Raeja I guess. I pretty much ignore all the other girls."

"At least you still pull them. You've got some serious charisma. I also don't see how you manage to be so straightforward, Mister, 'are you sure that's the only reason?' golly kid."

For the entire day I actually wasn't worried about whatever was happening. But I couldn't seem to shake the feeling that Raeja had disappeared because of me. I had sent her over the age, hadn't I? Then again, maybe she was just on a trip. I guessed I would wait it out.

The Tuscany girl had texted me, but I ignored her, I was not gonna attend a date with some random girl. I knew Alec would read the message if I left it there, so I deleted it.

This must've been how Raeja had felt when she went on a date with me. I wondered why she had gone, she clearly wasn't in the mood even before her whole sister fiasco. Ughhhh I was being so dumb. Every single thought I had somehow ended back up with something to do with Raeja. I needed to get over myself. She did accuse me of something I didn't do, she should be the one feeling bad.

Even after telling myself that, I couldn't get rid of the sense of dread.

Chapter Five

"I hate this freaking place. Why can't school just be over?" Alec was most certainly excited to be back.

Break had ended, and it was now Monday again. Everyone loves Mondays. Clearly. Alec, Cilisia, and I were standing in the math hall.

"You seem like you're just loving this, huh? Well GUESS WHAT?!" I made a fake shocked face. "...I have no idea. Don't ask me questions I don't have the answers to."

"I am so sorry professor handsomely." Alec said sardonically.

I put on my most professional voice, "As you should be.

You should keep up that description by the way. I like it."

Cilisia chimed in, "WOW, he's humble too."

During break, my sister got a navy blue dot, she was screaming after she saw it, and I swear, she burst my eardrum. Maybe even both of my eardrums. I made sure to wear long sleeves so she wouldn't see my color. She had asked about mine and I told her I hadn't gotten it and she didn't press further. I also managed to get away with telling Alec that Tuscany hadn't messaged me, I was more proud of that than I would've liked to admit, but most of all, I was preoccupied thinking of the one and only girly dearest, Raeja. Cilisia had tried to call her when she got her dot, and Raeja hadn't even answered then. If she was ignoring her best friend, something was definitely up.

I began responding with, "The most humble." Before I was cut off by a shriek. I turned to find Cilisia already a bit of the way down the hall, running to hug her best friend.

"OH MY GOD! RAE YOU'RE ALIVE!!" They hugged, Raeja winced on impact. Cilisia pulled back, scanning Raeja. "What the heck happened to you?! Why didn't you respond to me? It's been like... Since before the break." Raeja was an absolute mess, she looked like a zombie. Pale and her eye bags were dark. I thought I saw a bruise on her left cheek by her eye, but I could've been wrong. It was bad.

"I just fell down the stairs and my phone was in my pocket, it broke. Sorry." Raeja said.

Cilisia laughed. "You are such a klutz, that does not surprise me."

"I know right." Raeja looked over my sister's shoulder and we made eye contact. She looked pained, or maybe she had that look because I was there and she didn't like to see me anymore, and she could've just been tired from staying up at night thinking about her missing sister. I had done the same thing when my dad died. Unfortunately, I didn't actually think either of those were right. the state she was in was far worse, something else had to have happened.

The first period bell rang and Cilisia left quickly, her class was on the other side of the school and she didn't want to be late. Gotta keep her perfect student title.

Alec looked at me and leaned over to whisper, "You have got to talk to her, your sister is an idiot to believe that story. The chick looks like she was thrown off a three-story building."

"I know, I'll try and get the story out of her." He left.

I walked up to Raeja, bumping into multiple people who were flowing down the hall.

Raeja noticed me and turned to walk down the hall in the opposite direction. She had a slight limp. I caught up to her and she stopped walking.

"Are you okay? What actually happened? Falling down the stairs is not a great cover up story. Kind of lousy if I do say so myself, not that I know from experience or anything."

She looked at me, and for a second I thought she was going to tell me, but instead she shook me off.

"I have class." She started walking again.

I grabbed her arm to stop her and she snapped. "LEAVE ME ALONE!" I dropped her arm, wishing I could vanish. She stormed off, limp and all. I froze for a second before I went to class myself.

#

"Please Sis! Just ask her. She was totally faking that story." School had ended, and Cilisia and I were in the parking lot, walking to my car.

"First of all, why do you care what she says? And second, the story makes total sense, I mean, it was an entire flight of stairs. All of that could've easily happened. Why don't you believe her?" We were at the car now and she got in the passenger seat. I always drove.

"Will you just ask her?" I started the car.

"No, I have no reason to. I believe what she says, you can try and convince me otherwise, but until then I'm not asking."

"Ugh, fine." I explained how Raeja was acting at the party, and all of the accusation stuff, and about her sister, and I showed Cilsisia my dot. She was mind blown.

"I'm an idiot! How did I not notice she was acting completely off?! AND that you guys had the same dot. That feels so weird. Why didn't she tell me?"

I pulled out of the parking spot and started driving home. "I don't know. Don't ask me—"

Cilisia cut me off, finishing the sentence for me. "Questions you don't know the answer to. I get it."

"No, I was actually going to say that you shouldn't ask me, because you're her supposed best friend and all knowing."

"Yikes. Got me there. I'll talk to her I guess."

"Thank you." Finally my sister was helpful with something.

"Now tell me about this whole 'I'm in love with her' nonsense."

#

Two days later, Cilisia had all of the information, "She's a tough cookie, but I got her to crack. She literally made me swear on my life to not tell anyone. Twice. So you better make this worth it." She sat on the white couch next to me.

"Just tell me what happened."

"Why should I?"

"If you don't, I'll tell mom about that time that you snuck out to-"

She smacked her hand over my mouth. "Do not finish that sentence. I'll tell you. Basically, she only blamed you because there was not anyone to blame except herself. She told one of her colleagues from her internship about the illegal love stuff, somehow forgetting that she worked for the people who were literally directly connected and loyal to the government network. So she assumes they told, not you." She paused.

"Is that it?"

"No... I'm just reprocessing that she didn't tell *me* of all people. Whatever. Anywayyyyyyyysss, she went to look for any files of her sister at the police department and there was nothing there, so she decided to go to the records management facility, you know, the high security one they made after the system was established to keep all of the matches in order and that sort of thing.

"She tried to ask them if she could look for any files about Lindsey, but they said no and let her leave, then she went back two more times after that.

"She tried to sneak in after hours on her fourth try. But they didn't tolerate her after she tried to do that. She basically went ballistic and they called the police. She got detained in some secret prison. They had something over her head when she had first arrived so she didn't know where it was. Someone helped her get out, and she knows where it is now. I don't know how she got back here though. We assume that's where everyone who has disappeared is. Her parents also don't know about any of this because they thought she was staying at our house for the break." She rushed out the last sentence because she was out of breath.

"Holy bejeebers... That's wild."

"I know. She seems like such a softy: we have all been deceived."

"So... We just need to find her sister in an orderly manner and all will be well. Got it."

"Yeah, sure, I did forget to mention one itty bitty detail though."

"And what is that?"

"She said that the person who helped her was our dad."

Chapter Six

I could've sworn I was hallucinating. "I'm sorry, what? Our dad is *dead*."

"That's just what she told me, she's seen him before so it makes sense that she could recognize him. We have been best friends for like six years. This isn't something she would lie about."

"I know. But he's dead, so it can't make sense. We literally went to his funeral."

"His body wasn't there though. I think she could be right. I was thinking about it, and it actually adds up until a certain point. He worked for the government, right?"

I thought for a moment. "You're messing with me. It's not funny, you know?"

"I swear I'm not. I wouldn't stoop that low."

I felt like passing out. "I have no idea how that would ever add up."

"But maybe it does."

"Okay this little prank is going too far. Don't you have homework to do or something Princess Perfect?

"Nikko, I'm not lying. Think for a minute, he always came home and complained about how stupid his boss was. He hated the system, but his boss made it, so our dad knew basically everything about it and maybe he did something to tick his boss off. If they're doing something about other people that are marrying people they love, do you not think they'd get rid of someone who actually had some effect on the situation in a way that tons could revolt?"

I stood and began pacing. "He probably did do that. But what other context do we have?"

"Raeja said that he was there but I'm not sure how much she really knows about why he is there."

"Our dad is alive..." I said, mostly to myself, still not totally sure if it was some joke or not.

"Yeah, but Raeja also said that she heard them catch him when she escaped. He could be dying."

"Then why are we still here? Let's go get him."

"We will, but Raeja said she's coming too. She wants her sister back just as much as we want our dad. I already talked to her about it."

I raised my eyebrows. "I'm surprised she wants to go back to that place, and more surprised she is willing to go with her nemesis."

"You're not her nemesis, I already told you that."

"Sure you did." I didn't know if I believed that. "Now we need an escape plan. Maybe I'll tell mom we're going camping?"

"Uhhhh it's a school night," she noted.

"Frick, well, I guess we can say we're going to the library and having a study party."

Cilisia laughed. "You really think she is going to think *you* would go to the library for any reason?"

"Fair point. That one was mostly a joke. What do you suggest?"

"Let's just say we're going drop something off at Alec's or

something and just not come back."

"Alright."

#

Cilisia and I pulled up to Raeja's house about two hours later at 5:30, we were waiting for her in the driveway.

"She just texted me, she just had to convince her mom to let her come," Cilisia informed.

I swallowed hard. "Alright."

"Why are you so freaked out right now, breathe kid."

"I'm just still processing all of everything, it happened so fast."

"Right. This is a weird side of you. When Rae gets in the car, we are going to pretend like everything was normal, I don't want you guys to do your apology and mushy gushy stuff in front of me. You're literally made for each other, even the system agrees, but I don't want to hear it."

"I agree."

Cilisia pulled out her phone to message Raeja. "I'll tell her that as well."

Raeja walked out of the house a few minutes later, seeming a bit less zombie and a bit more human. She wasn't as pale and she seemed to have pulled herself together as best she could. She got in the back seat and Cilisia moved to the back to be by her friend.

I looked at Raeja in the rearview mirror. "What a weird change of events. Raeja, the girl who hated me this morning, is in my car and we are on our way to go save our family members. This would make a good book."

Cilisia smacked me on the back of my head. "I told you to save it you chum bag."

"Right, forgot. Where to, Rae?"

"It's in Lead, so just start going there and once we get close I'll give more specifics."

"Really that far? How the fetch did you get back here from there?"

"Busses."

"Right, obviously."

Lead was six hours from our house. My parents, Cilisia, and I had driven through it once on our way to Mount Rushmore because they got lost. We were probably eight when we went and I remember it being freaky as hell. It was basically abandoned and there was a huge mine that, at the time, I assumed was from a meteor. As an eight-year-old would. I didn't still think that. Definitely.

About two hours in, I asked Raeja, "Wait, is the prison thing in the mine? They stopped using it a long time ago didn't they?"

"Bingo."

"Wow, I have to give it to them, it's a good spot for secret detainment. Literally no one wants to go to Lead."

"Exactly, it's deep down there too, they were not messing around," Raeja said.

I glanced back, Cilisia was asleep against the window.

I sighed. "She literally always falls asleep in the car, I swear."

"Yeah, it's a long drive though, not like she's got anything else to do."

"Valid."

When we got to Lead, it was 12:48am. We had stopped for food at around seven and also stopped at a gas station to gas the car and have a bathroom break. The girls were both asleep when we got there and had been since at least 11. My mom had texted me maybe just shy of 22 times, I did answer about three of them, but after that point I decided ignorance was the best option at this point. I wondered if she'd think we died or something. My phone buzzed. *Mom.* "Oh frick," I said to myself. I wanted to answer so bad, but I couldn't.

When my sister was still sleeping earlier, Raeja and I took that as our opportunity to mend things. It went pretty well in my opinion.

I pulled into the mine's visitor center parking lot and decided to look up what this mine actually was and see what popped up. The first site that came up read:

`The Homestake Mine in Lead, South Dakota, was once one of the largest and deepest gold mines in North America. While the mine is no longer operational, its historical significance is still evident in the landscape. It is now the location of the Deep Underground Science and Engineering Laboratory.`

"So comforting to know it's that deep," I whispered. I had no idea how we were going to pull this off. "Guys, wake up." I turned and shook Cilisia.

She rubbed her eyes. "Are we here?"

"Yup, home sweet home. Wake Raeja up, I'm gonna go get the backpack out of the trunk." I got out of the car and walked around to the trunk. My mom had put together a small hiking backpack with a first aid kit, some random medications, and some snacks. She did pack it for camping purposes, but I thought I may as well bring it just in case.

The two girls got out of the car. Not looking so tired anymore.

Everything was dark and the town looked even more abandoned than I had remembered. I shivered when a cool breeze brushed my skin.

"I hate this place."

"Same," Raeja and Cilisia said in unison. They probably hated it for different reasons though. We walked over to the railing that warned us to stay out of the pit. It really was deep. It was dark outside too so it looked even worse. I managed to make out the shape of the mine. It was kind of a funnel with staircase-like ridges, at a point it just turned into an abyss though.

"What's the game plan Raeja? You've been in this place before."

"Well, the door to the prison is on the side of the hole at the bottom. Well, the bottom of what we can see above ground, I'm not sure if it goes to the actual mining area. I got out by this dirt road thing they have going up it."

"Are we just going to walk that?" I asked.

"We can, but we might get killed before we get to the bottom. Your dad made a good diversion so no one noticed that I was also missing when I got out. I think it's a good idea to go right now, I'm just now sure how to do it without dying. The door is heavily guarded."

"Do they have a lot of cameras everywhere?" Cilisia asked.

"Where the door is, yes. I assume they didn't want to be too suspicious so they don't have cameras going throughout the entire hole."

"They're sneaky," Cilisia said.

"That was the goal," Raeja mentioned. "I think we should become real spies, being sneaky sounds fun."

I huffed. "Guys, stay on task. I think we just stay low and take it as it comes, we can g-" I was cut off by a loud explosion that shook the ground beneath us. "Holy flip," I exclaimed as I watched the sinkhole below light up.

An entire side of the funnel wall fell in, filling in a lot of what we could see. Cilisia screamed and Raeja starred in terror. After a few seconds she looked like she was going to pass out. I walked over to help her keep her balance, just in case.

"My-my sister was in there." She fumbled on her words.

"It's okay, I'm sure she's fine, just breathe," I said. She turned to hug me.

A few moments later Cilisia said, "Uh, guys, some kind of cult is coming towards us from the mine."

I let go of Raeja and turned to find a group of four tattered people emerging over the edge of the mine. It kind of looked like an apocalypse, they all wore bright orange jumpsuits and were out of breath. Two held flashlights, one had a taser or something. We stepped back a few feet from the railing and I slid in front of my sister and Raeja.

The first person jumped over the railing and I saw the outline of my dad. My actual dad, alive.

I tried to figure out if that was truly him. He approached me as another person in the group hopped the fence. The moment the figure's feet were on the ground, Raeja recognized her.

"LINDSEY!" Raeja ran to hug her sister, I tried to stop her but she wasn't going to let me. I let it slide for now, hoping she had good instincts.

"What happened to you girl?" I heard Lindsey ask after a moment, I blocked out whatever followed.

I turned back to the oncoming man and Cilisia slipped past me as well, embracing our dad. I decided it was him and joined her.

"Yo, Kael, you know these kids?" someone asked. My dad's old assistant, Hunter, stood about five feet from us.

Our dad pulled away. "Of course I know these kids, you idiot. Have I not talked about them every day since we were put in this dump? You've even met them."

"Ohhhhh they're *your* kids. Sorry, I didn't recognize them, they're not what I remember."

"Yeah, they are pretty big. But I would know them

anywhere." He hugged us again. His right eye was swollen shut and he now rocked a scraggly, gray and white peppered beard.

I couldn't help but ask, "Was that explosion yours?"

My dad nodded. "Yep, I thought we had more time than we did, otherwise we would've been out long before that."

"Welp, saved us some effort. Why were you here to begin with?"

"I opposed the creation of the system. They told me I had to oblige, but I continued to object and I told them that I would do everything in my power to get the country to hate them if they implemented it, so they threw me and my assistant out."

"Cilisia and I suspected as much," I said.

"You have always been smart."

"Apparently not smart enough. Only took us three years and a missing friend to find you. Then again, we weren't really looking until now. You were dead," Cilisia pointed out.

"Nah, legends never die." My dad said. "Although, they would've killed me if I hadn't blown the place. I did get your friend out and that wasn't too bad of a punishment, but still a punishment."

"Thank you for that by the way," Raeja said, walking over to us with her sister and the other guy that was with my dad.

"No big deal, only cost me yet another beating."

Raeja widened her eyes. "I'm so sorry."

"It really is fine, they were never going to get me to join them again anyways, dying wouldn't have been too awful for that cause." There was a pause.

"Hey, Rae, introduce me to this other guy you seem to

know," I suggested attempting to break the silence.

"I'm Jack, Lindsey's fiance." He stuck out his hand. I shook it.

"Nice to meet you Jack, I'm Nikko, Raeja's... friend."

Jack smiled. "Right, friennnnnd."

"Shut up," Lindsey said, slapping Jack's arm.

"I'm still confused how you guys managed all of this," Cilisia said.

"Your dad has been planning his escape for a long time, luckily, Lindsey and Jack are people he tolerates, so we brought them along," Hunter explained.

"How many people did you kill?!" Cilisia asked.

"Let's not worry about that sweetie. My plan still isn't finished so we can't headcount right now." Dad put his hand on my shoulder, "Who wants to kill the system with me?" We all agreed to help. "Alright, I'll call the jet, we need to get out of here before anyone shows up looking for us. Does anyone have a phone?"

Cilisia's jaw dropped, "WE HAVE A JET?!"

"Won't be the last thing you are surprised by. We have a whole corporation on our side that no one knew about."

"Our stuff is all in the car, my phone is in the cup holder in the front." I threw my dad the keys. "Do you need the password?"

"Nah. Let me show you guys how to hack a phone," My dad said.

I still had to get my brain to work out what had just happened, so I told them, "I'll come in a minute." And walked over to the other side of the visitors center. I found a bench and sat, the fatigue setting in.

Maybe a minute later Raeja came over to sit by me. "Hey, thanks for helping me out, even if they would've gotten out on their own."

"Yeah, no problem."

"You okay?"

"I'm great. But still confused by everything, everyone is so vague, or maybe I'm just tired and not picking up on some things."

"I get that. We can be confused after we shut this down though. We've got a lot of adventures to come." She kissed me on the cheek and walked away. My heart fluttered. She really was my soulmate, whether the system had agreed or not.

Countdown to Catastrophe

Lydia McClellan

My legs burned with every lunge, and beads of sweat dripped down my face. My head pounded as burning sunshine scorched my neck. It didn't help that I was wearing a suit, but I had to hurry, for the world depended on it.

As I approached my office building, I slammed into the towering glass doors, tripping over myself in the process. Then without even thinking, I stumbled right through security. A guard was sitting at the check-in booth, he was not in the best shape but he was committed to his job.

"Sir, sir, you need to sign in," The guard said as I continued to walk... he quickly stood up while saying, "SIR, if you do not listen to instructions you will be arrested. This area is only for staff." I stopped and turned to face him, reaching into my pocket. He looked startled thinking I was a threat. He watched carefully, preparing for the worst. I retrieved an ID... my work ID, the poor man seemed annoyed as he glanced over my ID before responding

"Next time if you choose not to check in I will arrest you even if you have an ID, do you understand, Mr. Jones?" I nodded before returning to my original course.

Entering the board room, I heard ten different people begin to talk fifteen different things at once, but my mind wasn't focused on them. My goal was to find the person who had summoned me with a cryptic text – Lesley Allred, my boss, the head of our program. Our system works for the government. We work in the lab, usually researching the molecular mechanism in nitrogen, carbon dioxide, the chemical fumes that are released from a car's exhaust system. Trying to purify the air to improve the air quality. Along with advertising 'organic options' that no one cares for.

But sometimes we do other things. This sounded like one of those things.

Leslie grabbed me by the arm the second I stumbled in.

"Even with such an alarming message, you don't seem to hurry very fast. Now will you please join me for a discussion? We have some important things to talk about... alone."

Ms. Allred excused me and herself out of the chaotic room without much suspicion. We started down the hall as she began to speak.

"Mr. Jones, finally... we just learned some information

about the 6GNCP which was just located farther into the earth's mantle than we ever thought was possible."

"Is it of any concern at the moment?"

"Mr. Jones," Lesley said as she came to a complete stop. "Did you just ask me if a planet-killing bomb was concerning? Obviously, it is concerning."

"But to what extent?" I asked as we began to walk down the hall once more.

"It is expected to be set off in 25 months, And if it is, the catastrophic explosion would end the world."

"I haven't seen any recording of it on the news."

"This is confidential information, there are maybe a hundred who know about it at this time."

"When will we tell the world?"

"We aren't going to tell them, less violence, and the world will end in peace."

"That seems so cruel –"

"Mr. Jones, don't let your emotions get in the way. I don't care what you have to say, it's been decided. No one, and I mean NO one is permitted to know. Stop looking at the floor and look at me... Do you understand?"

I gently looked up and nodded my head, not in agreement, but only because I knew there was no point in arguing. I completely zoned out. I couldn't help but think about my pregnant wife Jeanette and my little girl, Saylor. I always dreamed who she would grow up to be, and now her life was in jeopardy along with billions of others. And I couldn't tell anyone.

"Why am I being told this information?-"

"We have made a last-resort mission called IODOMUS." I definitely noticed that she ignored my question.

"And what might that be?"

"Essentially, transport as many people as possible to IO."

"IO? As in one of the moons of Jupiter?"

She ignored that. "IO doesn't currently have breathable air. But we could process the fumes and create oxygen and eventually live there permanently. And you would be somewhat helpful in that category."

I struggled to wrap my head around this. "If I remember correctly, that is 390.4 million mi away. This is impossible."

"If 6GNCP were to explode, the sonic field from the explosion could shoot a reserve capsule far enough to reach IO. But we would have to leave nearly everyone behind."

"How many people can we take?"

"We can complete 4 capsules in a year, and only 20 people can be supported in each one."

"Who is on the list?"

"The list isn't completed, but if you must know... you."

"ME?!"

"Yes, don't flatter yourself. It was mostly due to the fact that you have access to the government, and the PhD from Standard in biochemistry doesn't hurt your case."

"There are other PhDs," I said.

She stared at me for a moment. "So, you want me to tell them no?"

My cheeks got hot. "Well...no." Go to space? Would anyone of my generation ever say no to that?

But there had to be other options. "Can't we just turn 6GNCP off?" I asked.

"Obviously the software for it has a password, but finding it would be practically impossible. The institution that engineered this instrument is estimated to have advancements 20 years ahead of our technology. What we thought was the best tech we had."

"How do we even know this information? I assumed all we had was the blueprint. Honestly I'm surprised we haven't known about this for a while, the fact that 6GNCP was even built without any suspicion concerns me."

"Well, Mr. Jones...that isn't information I'm willing to tell you. Whoever created this institution knows what they're doing. Unless someone in this suicide institution told us the password, which isn't even an option–"

I interrupted. "From what I'm hearing, it's the only option. So tell me why it's supposedly impossible."

"You really think we could get one of them to answer a phone call?"

"WHAT OTHER OPTIONS DO WE HAVE, MISS ALLRED? WHY CAN'T WE AMBUSH THEM!" I clenched my fist, knowing I had stepped out of my place.

"Mr. Jones, I understand you are upset. But that doesn't mean you're allowed to react like a toddler. I am simply giving you the information that *you* asked for. How are we supposed to shut down an operation when we have no information about it?"

I tugged on my suit a bit and fixed it with my hair, slightly embarrassed.

"It seems we know a lot, it also seems like I'm being told half of what you know."

"You should be flattered, you know *this* much."

I wasn't flattered, It felt like half of the story wasn't being shared. This annoyed me, and she could definitely see it. I noticed her annoyance with the situation, but I couldn't understand why my boss wasn't devastated like me – did she have nothing to lose? I didn't know much about her or her personal life, other than the fact that she didn't wear a ring on her hand, and she was 25 as of two weeks ago. The only reason I knew that was because the office had thrown her a surprise party. We kept it pretty professional over the four years she had been my boss, maybe it was better that way. "Do we have an idea of how 6GNCP works?"

"In theory? Remember it was science fiction until this morning. I have blueprint papers in my office from the scan we made earlier today. Best guesses only."

"Great, I'm going to take those and then head home. Thank you for your time," I said with a fake smile as I turned around.

"My office is in the other direction, Mr. Jones."

"Right."

Miss Lesley Allred's office was futuristic, and stained-glass doors greeted me as they scanned my face. And a very animated computer lady with a British accent began to speak.

"My name is Kimmy Seona. How may I be of assistance, Mr. Christopher John Harrison Jones?"

"How do you know my full name? When did Ms. Allred put it in your system?"

"She didn't, your mom's Facebook account from 26 years ago posted you as an infant. She mentioned your name. Was I incorrect in my research, or should I do a deep dive on all your personal records that have been recorded in the government system?"

Stunned and, frankly, very unsettled, I stuttered back, "Th-that won't be necessary."

A subtle beep paused our rather confusing conversation and the doors opened, a strong aroma of luscious blossoms struck me. I cringed.

I whispered under my breath, "Someone likes Bath and Body Works."

The inside of Ms. Allred's office was very tidy and clean – black marble lined the floors, and LED light covered the ceiling. A small aquarium glowed on the right side of the room while a white pearlescent desk was on the left. It wasn't very personalized, except for a small picture frame on her desk. Being the nosy human that I am, I decided to investigate. Probably irresponsible but I don't care. I quickly ran over to her desk and grabbed the picture frame off of it, only to find a photo of a pretty lady in a white dress and a handsome groom next to her. She was so happy and her smile was so pure... it was Ms. Allred?!.

"I never knew she was married."

"Probably because I didn't want you to know," Ms. Allred said. Startled by her sudden appearance, I dropped the frame and the glass shattered.

"I hope you realize I could file this as vandalism..."

"But you won't, Ms. Allred. I vaguely remember you asking me to retrieve something from your office?"

"The model papers for 6GNCP." She skipped over the broken glass and opened her desk drawer to retrieve the papers,

"Why are we using papers, I think this could be sent through an email–"

"Papers can't be hacked Mr. Jones. We aren't sure what this institute is capable of." she smacked the papers on the desk, probably a little harder than necessary.

I ignored that, out of respect for the idea that she definitely didn't want me dead... Definitely. So carefully, I folded the delicate paper before placing it in my suit pocket.

"Mr. Christopher John Harrison Jones, Ms. Allred's heartbeat is rising and for your safety, it is suggested that you exit the premises," said Kimmy Seona before turning the LED lights red.

"Ms. Allred, I think your fancy AI thing is glitched. It called you Miss, not Mrs. Aren't you married?"

"I was married, I am not married anymore."

"Divorce rates are rising by the day."

"I wasn't divorced."

"Oh."

"One more thing. If you mention this situation *to anyone*, for any reason at all, your spot will be taken and given to someone else. Is that clear?"

"What about my wife?"

"Not even her. There are no exceptions." She paused, then said, "Is there anything else you are concerned about Mr. Jones?... Good, you may leave now, my patience is limited."

"Fine."

It usually only took me 12 minutes to get home... but not tonight. I took a deep breath before walking to the front door of my house. This house was the first home my wife and I had purchased. It was a little old cottage house built in the 1960s. It was a cozy home with a vintage feel to it. marigolds surrounded the entrance, the ones my wife loved to plant in the spring. The house wasn't fancy but I loved it, and the people in it.

"Dad's home" a spunky little girl with snarly brunette hair said as she ran across the room to tug on my suit, cuing me to pick her up and give her a big hug.

"How was your day daddy?"

I chuckled slightly, "Really boring, I bet you had a funner day."

"Dad, did you get a degree at Stanford?"

"Yes?"

"Then you should know that funner isn't a word...I'm disappointed in you."

"You're right, you must be smarter than me-"

"Oh Dad, I def-fin-et-tilly am."

I gently set my daughter Saylor down as my wife walked in, wearing a dirty apron that barely fit over her swollen belly, and some old slippers. Her dirty blonde hair was messy and her emerald green eyes were tired but she looked effortlessly perfect. She smirked before saying, "You're home! Took you long enough. Lucky for you we've been waiting to start dinner."

"I appreciate that," I said as I walked over to my wonderful wife Jeanette to give her a kiss.

My six-year-old, disgusted, covered her eyes and said, "Eww, I don't know if I can eat food anymore."

"Oh really, guess there will be more cake for your dad and me," Jeanette said as she gave me another kiss.

After another disgusted look Saylor replied, "I think I can survive, just for the cake."

"Sounds great Saylor, why don't you go set all the forks on the table for the spaghetti," Jeanette said.

"Fine," Saylor replied as she slowly excused herself out of the room.

"What's wrong?" my wife said as soon as Saylor left.

"Nothing, it was just a long day."

"Okay? Let's eat dinner, I guarantee Saylor is losing her patience. Can I take your blazer for you?"

"I would love that." I slipped my blazer off and walked to the kitchen.

Saylor *had* lost her patience, just as my wife said she would. and was now using the forks as combs to brush her snarly hair like Ariel from the *Little Mermaid*. I smiled at her, finding her creativity hilarious.

"Maybe we should let the forks be for eating, don't you agree?"

"No."

"Okay, well for tonight we're using them to eat our food."

"No."

"Okay Saylor, if we aren't going to use forks, how do you plan to eat your spaghetti?"

"A spoon." I broke out in laughter not realizing she was being serious, very serious. She paused our conversation with a glare, this is the moment my wife walked in. I looked at her only to see fear, that's when I noticed the paper she was holding...they were the same papers Ms. Allred had given me. The 6GNCP model papers.

"What are these, Chris?"

I sighed. "Let me explain."

1 year later

We had learned a lot this past year about 6GNCP. Apparently 6GNCP wasn't a bomb that was diffused, it used chemicals, not ones that we have seen in this combination before...such that new molecular organisms were created. All of this was protected by some sort of coded force field. We discovered this by attempting to dig deep enough to reach 6GNCP and shut it off manually. But the farther we dug the more complications we encountered, there were many occasions where machines stopped working and shut off due to some sort of directed electromagnetic pulse. Decoding 6GNCP was even more problematic. Trying to untangle its coded layers would take years. Everything we tried, failed.

Not only that, it seemed that our government was failing. The economy was falling apart. With the world in chaos, all I could do was prepare for the worst-case scenario. All *we* could do. There was always the shadow of my survival, lying between me and Jeanette.

I walked into the living room. Saylor was sitting on the couch being consumed by the comfy cushions, watching a show. I glanced over, to see what she was watching. *Frozen, Cinderella, Sleeping Beauty*? But to my surprise it was none of these, it was the news. I sat next to my little daughter as we watched a very well-dressed lady say, "An institution called The blackMord has just been exposed for planting a chemical bomb known as 6GNCP, which will be set off in 1 month..."

My thoughts raced – this announcement would cause rioting. Was it a leak? Did the government do this on purpose? it couldn't be possible that the government would leave the world in so much sadness and depression before it was destroyed. I grabbed the remote and turned off the TV, Saylor complained, still wanting to watch her show. I stood up, shaking. It seemed so real now that the world knew, my heart ached.

"Dad –"

"Not now Saylor."

"Why—"

"NOT RIGHT NOW," I said. Saylor's eyes filled with tears. I hardly ever got mad at her. I went to comfort her, feeling terrible for lashing out, but she jerked away and ran into her room. I thought about talking to her, but she probably wanted to be alone. Now standing by myself in a quiet room I noticed a mumbling coming from the kitchen.

Walking into the kitchen, I saw my wife in tears, she had already known about the situation ever since she found the model papers. Hearing it shattered reality, I went over to talk to her only to see sadness and regret in her beautiful eyes. I also felt a lot of regret, there were so many things I wanted to do with my life and so, so, so many things I never should've said. And now I only had 1 months. I gently pulled Jeanette into a hug, but then I remembered I had left Saylor in her room alone.

I apologized to Saylor for the way I acted before offering to take to get ice cream, and I watched her light up with glee as we climbed in my car and headed to the local shop.

I wondered if, after the announcement, they would even still be open. Upon our arrival they were not. Saylor slightly nudged me toward the donut shop which was right next door, as a replacement for the ice cream. Approaching the donut shop I noticed Ms. Allred in an alley way, she wasn't alone. A hooded figure was standing beside her. I wouldn't have thought much of it, but Lesley was in the process of handing him papers. Were they the blueprints?

25 days later...

Unlike most mornings I didn't have work, my boss wanted everyone to take turns spending quality time at home. Before we prepare to launch to IO. Since there were only 1 day until the launch, I wanted to spend some quality time with my wife. Unluckily for me my wife and Saylor had girl plans with her sister and niece that were arranged months prior. Therefore the only reasonable thing to do was to make a bagel, you see, the process was quite difficult. Taking the packaged bagel from the pantry and placing it in the well-loved toaster, was the prime of my existence, creating the best charcoal texture.

While I waited for my bagel to toast, I walked to the living room and sat in my favorite black leather recliner, the moment I sat, I thought about my experience at the donut shop. Was I hallucinating? Ms. Allred had been loyal for years, would she risk her carrier? Would she really be this cruel to want to end the world? There were so many questions, but all of them flooded out when the lights started to flicker for a second and then shut off. The door swung open. A bruised and scarred lady staggered in, mumbling. It took a second to identify her...she was a complete mess. But once I looked closer I realized it was my wife.

"Jeanette!" I rushed over to help her but she held up her hand in defiance.

"Don't. Leave me alone."

I was bewildered. "Jeanette? What happened?"

"I'm so sorry!" she said in between sobs.

"What? Why?"

"I know the password to 6GNCP."

"What?! How long have you known this?"

"I'm a member of the blackMord." She covered her eyes with her bloody hands.

I stared. "What?" I whispered hoarsely.

"I'm so sorry–" My wife was cut off by a loud explosion coming from the kitchen. I assumed it was the toaster so I ignored it. A tear dripped down my face. "How could you do this to our family."

"I didn't have a choice," she said begging for my mercy.

"There's always a choice." Anger and fear overcame me as I stared at my wife. A hooded figure stepped into our home. Fear struck me, was it the hooded man with Ms. Allred? A loud shot sounded, the figure dropped the gun and ran out the door. Jeanette fell to the floor, immediately I rushed over to her, a pool of blood soaked her shirt. I knelt beside her as tears streamed down my face.

"J-Jeanette. W-What happened?"

"PCNG6." Her lips barely moved as she forced out the word.

"What?" I leaned closer and I pulled her onto my lap, cradling her head in my hands.

"That's the password. She took a deep shaky breath. "I love you."

"Jenette, please don't go. Hold on."

"I am so sorry."

"No. You're not going. It's not your time."

"You have to let me go, Chris. Take care of Saylor. Tell her I love her."

"No!" I sobbed as she took her last breath.

I held her limp body close to mine. My tears fell on her face.

Blue and red lights flashed through the window, who called the police? A parade of officers slammed in my door, staring at me and Jeanette. And I knew exactly what they were thinking.

"Christopher John Harrison Jones, a mass murderer, killed his wife... how lovely."

"I didn't kill her." I said as I started to grab the sides of that steel cold chair, I was so frustrated with the fact that no one would believe me.

"OOOHHHH, but you did."

"Someone else stabbed her Micheal, why don't you believe me." After I said this he turned his face away looking into the distance.

"My name is Mr. Patch, you aren't allowed to call me Michael anymore.

Mounds of regret hit me at this moment, no one trusted me. There was no hope for me, I was going to die a criminal. After a few more questions he left, and I was stuck with my thoughts. I wasn't actually proven guilty but I was the only suspect and there was no time for a jury. So everyone would always believe I was a murderer. A few moments later the door creak open, in response my head shot up, the quick reflex left me dizzy and my eyes dazed.

A familiar looking women peaked her head through the door, who could it be...my wife?

"Mr. Jones I don't have time for this, but we need to get you on that space shuttle."

"LESLEY?!, what are you doing here?"

"Removing you from the interrogation room."

"Really?" I stood up, tipping over the chair.

"Your fingerprints aren't on the gun that was shot, but we only have 2 hours till launch off. So we are leaving."

"Okay, but why are you here."

"To save the world," Lesley said

To be continued...

Keeper of the Source Orchid

Savanna McClellan

Prologue

Walking down the hall of Anemone, the most prestigious school in all of the first realm, I felt a hand brush against my shoulder. Smiling, I turned to face Samuel. His hand ran down my arm for a second then fell to his side. The motion gave me goosebumps.

I felt something drop into my pocket. Picking it up I found a necklace with a rose stone on the chain. It must have cost a fortune, they were extremely rare because mining them was almost impossible. Dwarfs and their magic were the only ones who could mine them without having the fumes intoxicate them. "Mr Merrrrr, it appears you have dropped something."

Sam blushed. "I found it at the market and thought you might like it."

"Thanks."

With that confirmation I dropped it back into my pocket. I blushed the tiniest bit. His deep brown eyes were popping with mischief, everything was normal except . . .

"Your shirt is tucked in! I didn't know you were capable of even thinking about it!" I gave him the best astonished face I could muster.

He looked away before his face could show any sign of laughter. Moments passed by before he returned to face me. He showed no emotion but stern upright stiffness, or at least he was trying to.

"What is wrong with the way I'm wearing my uniform, Miss Bendal?"

"Oh nothing, Mr Merrrrr, just that you are doing a terrible job of covering your smirk." breathing hard and trying my absolute hardest not to laugh, I delivered the blow.

"Excuse me, Miss Bendal–" He cut off there. No longer able to keep a straight face, he burst into laughter.

Once the chuckling subsided we started towards our first class of the day.

Chimes rang throughout the school, echoing through the classroom telling everyone that lunch had started. Standing up from my desk I made my way trying to squeeze through the hoard of prodigies who were swarming the door out of the classroom, nope there was absolutely no way to get past them, time to go backward. Turning around was a struggle but when I finally managed it I could clearly see that I was barricaded in by many others. I'd have to wait with the crowd.

Finally arriving at the cafeteria I made my way to the lunch line. The room itself had a light-yellow hue to the walls, the floor was white tiles and rows of horizontal tables filled most of the empty space. At one of the tables sat the new exchange student, a satyr, hm maybe I'll go talk to her.

The lunch ladies behind the counter filled empty bowls or plates with new vibrant fruits and other foods. *Crucrem* pastry lined one plate, its delicious pudding-like cream could be seen falling out of the inside of the light fluffy bread. My hand drifted towards it when another hand pressed against my shoulder. Sam tapped my shoulder once more then went to his seat. Quickly grabbing my food I made my way to his table, it was in the back and no one else sat there.

"Good table choice, now what did you want to talk to me about?"

"Well....." His genuine hesitation worried me slightly, what was so important? "I heard a rumor that someone is gonna bomb the school."

I forced a laugh. "Ha ha very funny, you got me! I fell for...... wait, you're serious?"

Sighing he replied, "I know how it sounds but I wouldn't have told you if I didn't think it were true."

I wanted to speak but the intensity of his stare begged me to believe him.

"Kie look at me."

Looking up into his eyes I could see the sincerity of his words, and that was terrifying.

"Remember it is a rumor, that may not be true....."

"You told the Headmistress, right? This is pretty serious."

He shrugged. "I went right to her. But she wouldn't listen. She says this kind of rumor comes around all the time."

"But–"

"We might want to go outside for a little while, skip class, just to be safe."

"Wait, how do you know when it's happening?"

"I–"

Chimes rang once again, announcing the end of lunch.

Sam moved away from his half-eaten lunch and off of the bench, indicating for me to come with him.

"Sam, stop, you're freaking me out, what's going on! You were totally fine this morning. Why are you all the sudden freaked out?"

"We have to go now."

"But—"

Sam didn't wait for my reply, he took my hand and ran for the door. I briefly looked down at our hands, our fingers were intertwined.

I could feel my cheeks turning pink, ugh! I knew that it didn't have anything to do with him liking me, but it still made my heart flutter, and my fingers tingle.

Be cool, be cool, be cool.

Any 14-year-old girl who got to hold their best guy friend's hand would be turning pink too, but because of the situation I brushed the thought aside. Looking up I could see Sam surveying the room for the best possible route out. We locked eyes, and I could see his embarrassment at holding my hand. At least he thought it was weird too.

A tremor shook the ground, and a loud echo of a bomb roared across the entire building. At this point kids everywhere were screaming and running for doors.

Others looked frantic and just stood there, but Sam had his eyes on one thing, the door. His sprint turned into a desperate run as we neared the door, we made it! A massive wave hit my back, the motion was so intense, Sam's hand let go of mine, my vision blurred at the impact, flames danced around me. The wall I had hit looked like it was spinning, where was I? Why did my body hurt so much?

SAM.

At the thought my consciousness returned to me in full, I strained to get up. I could feel the throbbing pain in my left leg and arm.

Fire was everywhere. The once light walls were charred, the hall no longer had any roofs or walls, all I could see was the remains of the school. Scanning what was left over of the hall all I could see was fire and blackened stone and... there! Tears spilled from my eyes as I saw a black charred body among the fire, sprinting to it, I quickly fumbled to pull it out of the flames.

Once it was a good distance away I finally brought myself to look at him. I could no longer hold it in, my best friend was gone, burned to the point where no one could recognize him. My sobs filled the empty silence, time passed by in a blur, when my tears finally ran dry I looked towards his body once more.

"I promise Sam that I will find who did this to you, even if it takes years, I won't stop until I figure out what happened here and why."

Chapter: 1

5 years later

I was on the top floor of a sixteen-story building.

Dark halls were quiet, the clear crisp scent had a tang of dust to it. Being on the highest level of the building meant I had to be as quiet as possible, with the soft cold tile cracked and splintered it wasn't going to be easy. I silently prayed the book would be here, the gnomes were gonna kill me if I ransacked one more library. Two years ago, I had started going to libraries for the answers that nothing and no one else could give me. 62 libraries ago I discovered that only one book could give me answers on who had bombed my school 5 years ago. Once again I prayed that this would be my successful mission.

My shoes were made up of almost all cloth with little protection to my actual foot, I couldn't complain it made me 10 times quieter. Sharp pain shot through my foot, it lasted for a second then turned dull, lifting my foot I found a shard of jagged wood right in the soft spot, I pulled it out fast. I'd have to be more careful. I bounced, sprang and tiptoed through the mess. As I got closer to the far door I could see patterns painted delicately on an uncracked floor. Odd. I groaned, odd never meant anything good.

The first symbol was a frog, wait, all of them were animals, whoever created this place had to be a gnome, their nature powers allowed them to do many things but if this did what I thought it was going to do this was no normal gnome. Preparing myself mentally and physically I stepped on a squirrel on the far right, nothing happened. Next my foot landed on a flamingo near the center of the hall, again nothing happened. This continued for five more steps on a bear, a porcupine, a dog, a mouse, and a snake. Reaching the door I looked back once more at the strange animals, I'd deal with them on my way out.

The door was a heavy metal and its handle was locked with no visible key. Taking a bobby pin out of my pristine bun which was now a little messy I quickly unlocked and opened the door. A larger hall with long rows of books laid inside of the door, the dust was much more potent in here and you could barely read the titles. That's it? They're just gonna let me waltz in here and take their clearly hidden stuff? I glanced at the animal tiles again, suddenly understanding, their job isn't to keep people out, it is to keep people in, at least that made the most sense. That was kinda disturbing to know, why lock them in with most of your valuable information? It still puzzled me. *I guess I'll just have to find out.*

I started my search on the books, ***Spells and tricks for young dragons***, THE ART OF NATURE, **how to teach young ones of any kind,** **The forbidden secrets to the dragon breeding process.** ew! Why would they make that a book? This went on for more than 30 books, there had to be something else here.

Tricky but Useful Flying Tips flew off the

shelf as my elbow hit it with a decent amount of force. Picking it up I placed it back in, wait, I pulled it back out again fast, right behind it a lever stuck out of the wall! Finally, at this point I was about to die of boredom. I pulled the lever without a second thought, a clicking noise, turning noise sprung through the walls, then a book popped out of its place revealing a hidden nook, i had already passed that book! And looked all around it! Grumbling, I set off towards the small opening, it was the first one by the door. The book that had fallen was ***Spells and tricks for young dragons.*** Opening the book I found a space with a key in one of the pages.

I made my way to the nook, inside was a keyhole, finally something was going right today! I put the key in and in seconds it disappeared into the hole. Moments later a big thick book was pushed off the shelf, `Picky pocky pick pock,` behind it on the shelf was a good-sized book, I grabbed it and right on cue an alarm sprung from a hidden speaker, I opened the door to the room and stepped on the first animal without thinking.

A flamingo popped out of the tile, in a desperate sprint I stepped on the bear, the dog, the wolf, and the frog. Each one sprouted the same animal, only life-size and angry! Sighing, I sprinted for the balcony on the far end of the hall while the menagerie of animals gave chase. I dodged the bear which in return dug its claws into my shoulder, the wolf decided a nip at my shins was a warm welcome. The frog was by far the worst of them all, it reached out and stuck its slimy legs on my neck and slowly made its way down my back. My run faltered as I screamed for it to get off, using my hands I tossed it onto the wall. Finally at the balcony I looked back at the menagerie and said a not so sorry goodbye.

I jumped out and for a second I was weightless then I was in the starcruiser, my transportation. The streets of Sylvan Vale were silent, a small gnome town off the coast of the big cities. As the starcruiser lifted off and was about to rocket into space the unsettling feeling of being watched crept up my spine. Scanning the street I saw a shadowy figure slinking in the background. Who was out on the streets at 3 am? Crazies, that's who, I decided I wouldn't worry about it as the starcruiser reached space then cruised for a while and headed back down to my house, all that mattered was that I had the book.

Morning light filtered through my window. barely awake I checked my clock, 8:00 am! already! It seemed minutes ago that the book search had occurred. Excitement sparked through me, the book! I jumped out of bed and opened my side drawer, the safe inside snapped open after I entered the code. Inside laid the book, it being light out I could clearly see how fragile the good-sized leather book was.

I sat on my bed, the rough leather was soft under my prying fingers, there were intricate designs lining the edge embedded into the leather, a metal lock held the book closed, where was the key? My fingers traced the binding of the book, bingo! Right there was a small wooden key, it was tiny enough to fit in the hole. I pushed one end and the key popped out. I put the key into the lock and twisted it.

A clicking sound came from the lock, the leather binding came apart.

I took a deep breath. The excitement I was feeling was dizzying. I opened the book. The first page held a note.

If you have found this book, I am probably gone. The book you are holding right now and about to read holds secrets that need to stay unknown. Since you have already gone to all the trouble to get this book, I suppose you think I'm crazy for suggesting this. And you also may be wondering who I am. For those who are not smart enough to figure it out, my name is Kaneray Luri Luray Zumarlo Reiiokoli. And for those who are stupid and don't know me I am the most powerful gnome and maybe being in all the realms.

I spent my whole life dedicating myself to magic and to becoming one with the earth. Now that I have achieved those things I understand something of great importance, something that you could never understand without experience. This note is not here to tell you not to do something you are obviously going to do, it is here to warn you about the choice you are about to make.

The information in this book is even beyond me, but because I am almost all magic at this point, I have adjusted this book for the person who reads it. You might understand this when you try to start reading, or you will never understand it, it all comes down to you. See you soon!

P.s you might want to be a little careful while deciding whether or not you're going to read this book, ask yourself why you want it.

Your new mentor

K.   L.L.Z.R

Kaneray! She's real! I'm reading one of her books! She's like the biggest legend in gnomish history, and around the realms!. The thought made me dizzy, I couldn't believe it. Realization kicked in seconds later, what was she talking about this book having secrets, or about understanding it? My thoughts strayed uncontrollably, imagine the history! All the places it will describe! All the answers I'll get!

HOLD ON!

What was I getting into? I needed to think things over, and not give into my weaknesses! It clearly states the danger of these secrets getting out. Ugh! My curiosity told me to peek, my obviously correctly working brain told me to think things through. But do I ever listen to my brain, not really, so why would I start now!

Shaking my head I cleared my thoughts, obviously this book had a spell to tempt people but why? So many questions and not enough answers. But…. then again the book has plenty of answers. Snap out of it! I shoved the book away from me, how was I supposed to do this? It clearly has a powerful want spell on it.

Thinking about it, I retrieved the book and read over the note once more, nothing… wait she specifically said be careful while choosing whether you want to read the book. That's it! You have to want it yourself not from the curse! Focusing, I took a breath, and tried to shove anything that had to do with the curse or wanting the book to the side. I asked myself the simple question "why do I want the book?"

"For Sam, my best friend," I said aloud. Saying the words brought sorrow and affection for my lost friend. *So I can find out who killed him, so I can know why any wretched person would want to bomb a school.*

So I can finally be at peace with the fact that he's gone.

The truth hurt, and with that realization that I would not allow it to enter my mind for all those years, I sobbed, all the emotions that I had bundled up over the years with hate were now coming out, all the sad unbearable nights where I cried myself to sleep. All the times my parents tried to comfort me in my grief. All because someone had been soulless enough to bomb a school. If that thought had never arisen I might still be sobbing, but that was good, I needed that hate to cover and hide my grief, sorrow and loneliness.

Without realizing it, I had turned the second page to the book. I wiped my tears away. This was real, this had happened. Time to go get some answers.

Chapter: 2

The book contained nothing, what? I flipped through the pages, where were the answers she'd promised? I reached the last page and there was the note.

It seems my first curse did not stop you from reading my book, clever as you are to have figured out my first riddle there are still many others to come, and my book may be of some rather good assistance. The only way you are reading this now is if you followed my clue and outsmarted the book, congratulations, now prepare for some awakening news. This book was specially designed by me, so I didn't make it easy. The emotions you used to pass the trial were the book's way of telling what you truly desire. You will find all the pages empty except for the answers you desired most.

These answers will vary every time you open the book, and yes you will have to go through that terrible process again. And once again because this book is magic, my notes will appear on pages that you thought were blank, I suggest you read them for further instruction.

Your Mentor

K. L.L.Z.R

The moment the note said there might be others, I had immediately paused to check the book. Aha! The title The Sixth Realm. The sixth realm? There was no such thing as the sixth realm, was there? My eyes drifted towards the title, time to see how much Kaneray knows.

The Sixth Realm

Curently the sixth realm is considered a myth, not many elfians or any of the intelligent species know or have even heard of the myth. This is good because the sixth Realm was never supposed to exist. The Sixth Realm was not a part of the original 5, someone had to have created it, who it is unknown to me. What I do know is the sixth Realm is a fake realm, they used that name as a cover up, the reason why is not known to me. Though their true name is, The society of The Black Orchid.

I have now answered your first question/want, time for the second one, why would the Black Orchid choose to bomb your school?

Wait, how did she know I wanted to figure out why? It was almost like she was actually talking to me, like she knew I was reading her book. It puzzled me, how was that possible? What type of magic was needed to make a book this powerful? Back to what's important.

There are many things that are still a mystery to me, but what I have figured out is that The Society is playing some sort of blame game. They bombed your school and blamed it on the 4th Realm, which started the war we are in currnetly, The Lyfussian War. They were also the ones to start The Nafunnan War. And that for them was a small accomplishment.

The Nafunnan War. Realization hit me hard. The biggest bloodiest war in history fought by the Dragons and the Demons was provoked by the Society of the Black Orchid. And they thought that was small? Millions died, the Demon population almost went extinct. What kind of ememy would be so heartless as to bomb a school and start two devestating wars?

These were only some of the things I know about them, but this has answered your two questions. I'm going to share one more piece of information, they know you have this book. You must use the spell to hide it. I suggest you go into hiding as I did when they sent an assassin after me. Be careful, I tried to warn you, but know you are in too deep. You are now the only living thing besides me who knows the truth. I will give you more answers in time, but for now focus on staying alive so you can end this war and wars to come. So you can avenge Sam.

The Visitrin spell

Ingredients

- One lilyurn petal
- Five chestle moon pades
- A teaspoon of cowcine
- Four leaves from a wallow crinel
- Two tablespoons Saliva from a sorunim
- Three tablespoons Lyinal

Recipe

Get a large pot, put the cowcine in and let boil, then slowly add sorunim, mix until bright yellow. In a separate bowl use a crush the wallow crinel, add a drop of the lyinal. Let sit. In another bowl chew the chestle moon pades with the lilyurn in your mouth then spit into the bowl. After going back to the pot, add in the rest of the lyinal by teaspoons, then as fast as you can add in the wallow crinel poltice, stir in well. Then SLOWLY add in the lillyurn poltice. DON'T STIR it. Take it quickly and pour it onto a plate (needs to be glass) at this point the liquid will be hardening fast so roll it into a ball. Put it into the fire/ hot oven for about 20 minutes (look away while in the fire/oven) take it out and use this spell with the marble in hand, make a password and say it to the book and the marble (make it memorable) then say Visitrin laborquenta nuquitle lighten and gone back and forth, disperse! If you need the book all you have to do is hold up the marble and say your password and blow on the marble.

Your Mentor

P.s good luck!

Excitement filled me, I always wanted to do a spell! The hard truth settled in, an assassin? I can't believe Kaneray is in hiding. Taking a deep breath, I proceeded with everything she had just said. I pulled my necklace out of its hiding place on my neck, and rubbed the rose stone that was given to me by Sam. New determination hit me. Time to get to work.

~.`~.`~.`~.`~

Hours later all the ingredients that were needed for this intricate recipe were found. And by the time I had finished the recipe itself it had taken up the better part of the day.

Sitting on my bed I looked out the big window in the center of my room

The view was beautiful, clear skies, a grassy meadow surrounded my house, and a cliff bordered the teal ocean. My bedroom had an ocean feel to it, teal walls, shells adorned the shelves, along with other things, my bed had beige covers with teal highlights.

A timer rang throughout the first 2 floors of my 4-tier house, me being on the third. When the timer finally reached me, I sprinted to the kitchen. Smoke filled the kitchen and the hall, the oven was smoking. I quickly pulled out a small crystal-clear marble, and I set it on the blue marbled counter. It was a very pretty color, but it had a forbidding aura to it. I went back to my bedroom and grabbed the book.

I flipped to the instructions. Ok make a password... What would be a good password? I thought about this for a good 20 minutes before it came to mind. Why not make it our initials S.T.M,K.R.B. Sameul Tyrain Merrrrr and Kiearra Roshein Bendal. That I could remember, I said the letters to the book and the marble then repeated the phrase "Visitrin laborquenta nuquitle lighten and gone, back and forth, disperse!" Very suddenly the book disappeared and all that was left was a marble. My expectations had been very high, and obviously I was disappointed. Sighing I put the marble in a hidden pocket in my purple fitted long-sleeve tunic, the white blouse I had underneath now slightly smelled of smoke, I wouldn't have to worry about the marble, there were plenty of pockets in my leggings and even some in my knee-high boots.

What next? All the excitement of doing the spell had distracted me from the actual warnings Kaneray had put in her book. Assassin? They wouldn't send an assassin after a 19-year-old girl. Would they? The terrifying thing was that I had no idea what they were capable of, I had no idea what they were willing to do.

Chapter: 3

A shiver ran down my spine, my legs burned with exhaustion and pain from running. My lungs were on fire from lack of oxygen. The void I was in seemed endless, and the person chasing me never seemed to give up. Breathing hard I looked to see my pursuer gaining on me. My emotions were like anarchy, and fear was the king.

I saw the pursuer's hand grab onto my arm, but I felt nothing. Right before I could get a good look at his face, everything vanished, and I opened what felt like my already open eyes. I was in my room, my covers flung to the side of the bed, my face and pillow drenched in sweat. I wiped my face with my sweaty T-shirt, and slowly got out of bed. As I headed to my bathroom I had the weirdest sensation that someone was watching me, like that night when I had stolen Kaneray's book.

Once again I let it slide off my shoulder. My bathroom was connected to my room, so when my feet touched the cold tile it gave me a shiver. I flipped the switch and having been in the dark this whole time it blurred my vision. Suddenly my feet slipped from under me and I was falling, my face hit the ground hard, I was too groggy to counter the attack. The loose braid I had in fell out and my long brunette hair fell around my face and shoulders. With a sudden motivation I flipped over and pinned my attacker, he wasn't expecting that. His dirty blond curls fell out of the hood he was wearing, so I pulled back.

My heart stopped, tears threatened me, but I would not budge. It couldn't be, there was no possible way, there was no way. My emotions went haywire, anger, hatred, longing, love, happiness, and so many more. But the ruler of them all was confusion. How could he do something like this? What was happening? He was supposed to be dead.

Finally I brought myself to look into his face, hoping and dreading what confirmation I might find. His eyes held sadness, terror, joy, and confusion. As I studied him a little longer the confirmation was there, this was Sam. The thought shook me and everything went black.

"Kie, Kie, Kie! Wake up."

A groan escaped my lips, where was I? The question answered itself as my memories came flooding back to me. Fully awake I looked straight at Sam. he stood right above me. He was close enough that I could easily pull off both, with no second thought I brought my knee into his crotch and my knuckles to his face. He shot away from me like a firework. Smirking with satisfaction and not an ounce of regret, I stood.

The wobbliness in my legs forced me to take it slow, and the rush to my head was not fun, but at least I was up. I looked towards Sam's sprawled body on the floor, I stood there with a look of boredness. When he finally recovered, his mouth opened, then shut. That's what I thought. The satisfaction was coming back.

"I guess I deserved that, but you don't need to look so smug about it"

"Oh yes I do! You deserve everything that's coming for you and more"

Once again his mouth opened, then closed. The victory was short lived, and the more serious question was earth shaking.

"You're supposed to be dead." the question hung in the air like a wasp, no one wanted to go near.

He swallowed. "I... Um... well..urgh.. It's a long story"

Expectantly I turned away and made my way to my bed, sat down and patted the space beside me.

"I've got time."

He looked even more uncomfortable as he sat on the bed, he obviously didn't want to do this.

"Start from the beginning and don't miss any details." I had been waiting for this for a long time.

Seeing that he obviously couldn't get out of this he started, "So my father works for a group called the Black Orchid—"

"THE BLACK ORCHID!" I threw myself off the bed into a shocked stance. How could he be with the Black Orchid, suddenly all the security I had by his homecoming was cut away by betrayal.

"Wait, how do you know what that is?"

I gulped nervously, he definitely shouldn't know about the book. "Um, there was something about it on the news." The fact that I had to lie was heartbreaking, but I still didn't know if I could trust him.

"Okay, do you want me to tell you or not?"

I fell back unto the bed. "Yes."

"Forewarning, I'm going to start from the beginning, I'm going to tell you everything I know, and no questions, okay?"

"Okay! Just get on with it."

"My father works for the Black Orchid, he met my mother outside of the organization, that is a huge rule to break, by the way. Then they had me, my father paid my mother to take me go and never come back. When I was really young my mom died of cancer, at that point I had to start living with my father, and that's when the organization decided to recruit me. They didn't like that my father had broken the rule but they saw potential in me—"

"Wait, wait, wait THEY HIRED YOU!?"

The look of excitement on his face had disappeared at my shocked reaction. Why was he excited?

"I...I thought you'd be...I don't know what I thought." The hurt on his face was heartbreaking.

"I'm sorry, please finish." I wanted to be furious at him, but...I wanted more answers.

"Ok, but if you didn't like that you're not gonna like what comes next."

I quickly mentally prepared myself for the worst, little did I know even that wasn't enough for what was coming.

Chapter: 4

"I was five years old when my mother died, when I lived with my father training was mandatory, that and school. I was 9 when we met and by that time I was almost out of spy school, having started at a young age. Normally young recruits are not allowed outside friends or relationships, but seeing that there was none my age they were merciful in our friendship. That rose stone necklace that I gave you was actually from the 3rd realm." He paused as if nervous then slowly continued.

"That day... when the school..." He swallowed

"Was... well bombed, I was trying to get you out because I knew it was gonna happen, they bombed it for a different purpose but used it as the excuse to get me out to fully focus on my training."

Tears brimmed my eyes, did he truly not understand that bombing a school full of innocent children was wrong? Was he truly beguiled by this so-called group?

"So—" my voice shaking "that... that body... that we buried—" My words broke off and were replaced with sobs. All the grief he had put me through came back like a waterfall drowning me. He pulled me closer into him, anger sprouted from me. Did he really think he could hug me right now? After everything he put me through? No. I pushed him away, our eyes met, and he could see my anger.

"I... I know what we did was... wrong, but it was for a bigger plan, a better purpose!"

He truly sounded as if he believed this nonsense, and that's what scared me. I stood up and moved cautiously towards the door. Could I even trust him? For all I knew this was all a trick, a scheme to kill me. A question bubbled in my mind, anger and betrayal followed it in rage.

"Why are you here?"

"Well... see...I didn't know it was you... and... I won't, but I didn't know—"

The truth dawned on me. "You're here to assassinate me." The revelation kicked instinct in. By the time I had caught up with my brain I was already behind a locked reinforced door.

"Kie, open the door, I can explain!"

"Who was he?"

"Who?"

"That boy that we buried!"

"Oh I don't know, just some kid killed by the bomb, why do you ask?"

What was happening to my so-called best friend? When did he become so sick that he didn't care about a living person? "WHY DO I ASK? When did you become so heartless to not care about a little boy! Saying it's all for a bigger plan, how can your society be good if they don't care about killing children!"

"It wasn't my choice! And either way he died for a purpose."

The hatred in my eyes was sparking through my words. ``Are you hearing yourself! He died because your group was so murderous to have bombed a school!"

"Stop, just stop, I can't talk to you right now." Tears spilled from my eyes as I walked away from my bedroom, Sam pleading for me to reconsider.

Chapter: 5

I had been sitting in the spare bedroom for more than two hours, my eyes were dry and no longer able to cry. Lost and confused, I got the only thing that could get me more answers. I stared at the book's leather wrapping, after having put in the password and the magic words I finally had the book. The same want from before was there but somehow dull, knowing the drill I got all my anger, devastation, and hurt together and slammed it onto the book. Flipping through the pages I found nothing, of course not until the last page.

Welcome back, as usual I thought I'd give you a little information before the big stuff. First of all congratulations on finding Sam!, second I am very sorry he's chosen the wrong side. It is getting more and more dangerous to use this book, you need to be careful when and where you pull it out. Now for the real deal, I know your friend is having a rough time deciding which side to choose but he better make up his mind and fast. I have a mission for you, you need to travel to the third realm, back to Sylvan Vale.

~.`~.`~.`~.`~

The door slid open at the slightest push of my hand, breathing on my shoulder reminded me of Sam's presence. It had taken us 3 whole days to travel to the outskirts of Sylvan Vale, I hoped it was worth it. The line of books was still there, but the place looked sacked. A shiver ran through me as I searched for the book I came to retrieve. There! The silver book with gold trimming lay underneath several books barely visible, picking it up I motioned for Sam to keep watch. Opening the book I felt a tingle run though my body, everything blurred, I wasn't in the library anymore, I was... I didn't know where I was. A silver door stood in front of me, the gold trimming looked exactly like the books. You would think there would be a room or a hall surrounding it but there was nothing but blur. The door opened and out came a scaly old body of a gnome, Kaneray!

"What? How?"

"Hush child, you have done a good work. I have waited 30,000 years for a successor, and you have finally come. To answer your question, The Black Orchid is not the organization I made it out to be. I have been in business with them for over 1,000 years, they have helped me try to decide a successor to protect the Source Orchid. You fit the profile, and it's about time, I am almost ready to go."

"Wait, so is Sam in on this?"

"Yes, though he somewhat ruined the plan, he also recommended you."

"I'm confused, did they actually bomb the school?"

Kaneray sighed. "We did not bomb the school, but another organization who is actually against us did, we just used it as an excuse to get Sam back for training and it benefited you as well."

"Benefited me, you call all my suffering a benefit?"

"Child, you must understand that The Black Orchid is not against us but there are others that are, my time is up and you must take my place. You will train with the organization for a few years then start your journey protecting the Orchid, and any other artifacts that are needed. What do you say?"

"Why me?"

"If not you then who?"

Taking a deep breath I could barely think about what this would mean for my future. "When do I start".

Epilogue

A smile spread across my face, as I walked down the aisle, Sam stood beside me our hands intertwined. We had finally finished training and could start our first mission next week. Ever since Kaneray had explained that I was the next protector of the artifacts it had been training and Sam, after a year we had started dating, and now we were married. Thankfully the organization had allowed us both to be the protectors, we had trained together ever since.

It had been 6 months since Kaneray's death, so we were very pressed to get started. I looked into Sam's eyes as we reached the end of the line where we were both pronounced graduated. We shared one last kiss before we left for our mission.

If Perfect is Worth It

Keaton Boyack

One

Fire was no stranger to Percy. His family was famous for being the masters of the elements. Which was why he was perfectly calm as the flame hurtled towards him. He stretched out his arm and absorbed the fire completely.

He could feel his arm heating up instantly from the fire trapped inside, and he knew he only had about a minute to shoot it out, so he began to run.

The obstacle course was easy, but still tedious. It was designed to slow people down so they wouldn't finish in time, with unnecessary ropes, beams, and lots of twists and turns.

But luckily, Percy rounded the corner with ten seconds to spare, and shot the fire back out. The target in front of him began to burn, and it turned blue, indicating the training was complete.

Percy wiped his forehead as he headed back to the main room, just as Walker headed out to the obstacle course.

He sat down on the hard bench across from his brother Aresto. "Are you going out after Walker?"

"I've already done it," Aresto replied. "I thought I'd wait for you."

Percy smiled. "Do you know what time we're supposed to meet with Cyclone?"

"In about an hour, I think. We should probably get home and change before we head over to Cyan City. I hear it's quite fancy."

Quite fancy was an understatement. Cyan City was the largest city in the Forgotten World, and it brought a new meaning to the word luxury. Jeweled fifty-foot-tall buildings, pink foliage all over the city to bring natural beauty to the streets, plus so many roads. It took them fifteen minutes alone to find the building they were looking for, and another ten to find the room that Cyclone was in.

For all twenty-five years of his life, Percy had lived in the countryside, with the beautiful scenery of the giant realm that was the Forgotten World. So he was quite overwhelmed in the sprawling city.

But they found it eventually, and Percy didn't know what to expect as Aresto pushed open the doors.

Sitting at the long desk across the room was an old man who looked like a wizard – long white hair, elaborate cloak – Percy wouldn't have been surprised if he had pulled out a wand and hexed them.

But instead, he waved to the three seats on the opposite side of the desk, indicating they should sit.

Aresto looked at the empty seat next to him. "Were you expecting someone else, Mr–"

"Please, just call me Cyclone," the man said. "And to answer your question, yes. There *was* someone else who was supposed to be here, but she canceled last-minute. Never really explained why…"

Percy cleared his throat. "I assume you'll tell us why we're here?"

"Of course," Cyclone said. "It's for the same reason that I have been against the Council for so long. You and I want change, and the Council is against it. So it's time for us to do something."

"And what do you propose?" Aresto asked. "Percy and I have been trying to think of things for years now, and nothing we have come up with fits the Council's policies. Everything is either too dangerous, or not effective enough."

"Believe me, I know," Cyclone said. "I have the same concerns as you do, and I have the same desire for a solution. But sometimes, people associate 'risky' with 'dangerous'. My plan might be a huge risk, but as a wise man once said, 'No risk, no reward'."

"And you're saying it wouldn't be dangerous?" Aresto attempted to clarify.

Cyclone hesitated. "In the wrong hands, it very well could be. But that's why I called you here. I know of your family, and I know how skilled you two are. I thought about inviting Walker too, but from what I hear, he can't be trusted to handle important things carefully enough."

"That is definitely true. And as a Councilor, I find it hard to believe he wouldn't report us," Percy said. "So what is this plan? Aresto and I are open to ideas."

Cyclone took a deep breath before answering. "For years I have been studying creatures' powers and what would happen if they were combined. I love experiments. All my childhood, I have been fascinated by things like this. What will happen if I pour this liquid into this other liquid? What will happen if I meld these two things together? What will happen if I combine two creatures?"

"So you're saying the right combination of creatures could result in something that could help the Forgotten World?" Aresto asked. "Something that could restore the Forgotten World's natural beauty?"

"Precisely," Cyclone said. "Creatures here have powers that can do wondrous things. But something extra must happen if two of those powers combine. And that is what I have been working on. I've been trying to find creatures with powers that, when they combine with each other, result in something that could bring the Forgotten World to a more pristine state."

"And you found it, didn't you?" Percy said, shifting forward in his seat and leaning in. "That's the only reason you would call us here *now* instead of any other time."

Cyclone smiled. "Indeed. But it's more complicated than you might think. I need *three* creatures instead of two. And combining three will be much harder than two. Also, these creatures are very rare and incredibly hard to capture. For this experiment, I need a phoenix, a griffin, and a dragon."

Percy's eyes widened. "Do you know how impossible those are to catch?"

"Not impossible, simply im*probable.* And that's why I called you here. I plan to get in touch with Vipera as soon as possible to bring her into this."

"Vipera?" Percy said. "Is she the one who canceled on you?"

"Yes, that's her," Cyclone said, obviously irritated. "But what I also know is that between you two and her, we have a very large network of important, *skilled* people. You two know a lot of people. So does she. So what I want is for you two to find as many people as you can who might be able to help. How about we meet back here in a week?"

"What should we tell them?" Percy asked.

"The same thing I told you just now," Cyclone said. "Bring them with you next week. I look forward to seeing you."

Two

"You realize the gravity of this situation you're dragging me into, don't you?" Archer asked, dragging a hand through his bright red hair. "This is basically illegal and we could get into serious trouble for doing this."

Percy sighed. "I understand. Bismarck Quiroz from Westclifia brought up the same concerns. But the Council hasn't been doing anything. They resist change like their life depends on it. The Forgotten World needs something to keep it beautiful."

"And these three creatures would?" Archer said.

"According to Cyclone, yes."

"What did Bismarck say?"

Percy frowned. "I don't believe it matters, but he said he'd give it a shot. His family supports the Council whole-heartedly, so he's having to hide this under an alias: Trevor Skybreaker."

Archer groaned. "I guess I'll try it? What do you even need me for anyway?"

"You are an expert in not only technological science – which will come in handy anyways – but animal physiology. You would be invaluable to us. Also, you have a lot of political power – you're very influential – and a lot of people listen to you."

"Fine. I'll try. But don't expect any sort of long-term commitment. Doing things this illegal could ruin my reputation."

"That's why we're in a time crunch," Percy said. "We need to make this creature quickly. The less time we spend doing illegal things under the Council's noses, the better."

"Have you gotten anyone else to join you?" Archer asked.

"Not aside from Bismarck, but I have a few more ideas. For now, just meet at the address I'll send you in Cyan City next Thursday evening."

Percy collapsed on his bed that evening as Aresto walked into the room. "Any luck?" he asked.

"Yes, actually," Aresto responded. "I got three people to join – Kai Andersen, Silas Ironfist, and Raven Thornwood."

Percy ran through his recent memories, trying to see if any of those names were familiar. "Isn't Kai Andersen the maker of that ability copying glove?"

Aresto nodded. "He's an extremely talented Technopath. Raven Thornwood is her own freelance battle force, and Silas Ironfist is a brilliant engineer. How about you?"

"I got four. Archer and Bismarck you know already, and then I got a pair of assassins – they're sisters – Aria and Jasmine Eldrosian."

"Why would we need assassins?"

"Why would we need a battle force?" Percy countered. "Caution, that's why. We're doing this completely illegally and could get severely punished if we get caught. Don't we need a way to defend ourselves if that happens? Plus, I'm sure all three of them have brilliant minds and could be very helpful."

"That's... fair, I guess," Aresto conceded. "You're doing it again, by the way."

Percy swore as he glanced at his hands, which were juggling a ball of lightning. He had manifested as an Electrokinetic quite late, and ever since then, he couldn't stop himself from playing with the electricity. It fascinated him. He had always wondered why electricity wasn't one of the elements.

"Do you know anything about this Vipera person?" Percy asked.

"Never heard of her in my life. Although from what Cyclone said, she could be very helpful."

Percy nodded slowly. "I guess. Do you think that trusting Cyclone is really a good idea?"

Aresto shrugged. "I don't see why not. He wants the same things we do, Percy. And, unlike us, he actually has a way to fix this."

Somehow, gathering everyone together that Thursday made it so much more *real* – as if it wasn't entirely real before.

Kai Andersen was strange, with his eyes, cloak, fingernails, and the tips of his hair all changing color at the same time. One moment, they'd be dark yellow, the next they'd be lavender, the next they'd be red, and they would just keep shifting through colors with no obvious pattern.

Silas Ironfist was a bit overeager. He said that he had been wanting to do something for quite some time, he just couldn't do anything by himself.

Raven Thornwood didn't look like a one-woman battle force, but Aresto assured everyone that she was very powerful and easily underestimated.

Vipera still did not arrive, and this time, Cyclone had no explanation for her absence, only claiming that she had said she would be there.

"I'm glad you two were able to recruit so many people," Cyclone said. "It appears we have a wide range of talents, which will be quite useful."

"Is there any sort of plan?" Silas asked. "A lead, a next step, something like that?"

"Yes. Our plan is quite simple. All we need to do is capture these three creatures, and I assure you, that will be the hardest part. From then on, it will be quite easy, what with the myriad of talents we have at our disposal. The one we're going after first is the griffin, the easiest to catch."

"Where are we going to find a griffin?" Raven said.

Cyclone smiled. "Not *where*, but *how*. And the answer to that is... we'll lure one out. Griffins love to hunt – they're predatory creatures. And my research has shown that they like to prey on their cousins, the hippogriffs."

"So we get a bunch of hippogriffs and hope a griffin comes?" Aria said. "Do you have a place in mind where we can find enough hippogriffs?"

"I can answer that," said a voice from the doorway, and almost as if it was rehearsed, everyone's heads spun around in unison to see who was talking.

It turned out to be a small woman with a white dress, long perfectly styled red hair, and an excessive amount of makeup. She strode into the room with an air of confidence and took the seat next to Aresto.

"You're Vipera?" Percy said.

"I am. And as I was saying, I know a group who use hippogriffs as their mounts. All we have to do is convince them to take their hippogriffs out, and a griffin is bound to come for food."

"How do we make them do that?" Kai Andersen said.

"We don't *make* them, we *convince* them. Tell them... there's a threat to their tower, something that needs to be hunted down, and they'll ride into 'battle' on their hippogriffs."

"What is this group?" said Jasmine.

"They're called the Skyborn Legion," Vipera said. "Their whole goal is to be recognized by the Interstellar Association as official knights."

"That's a thing?" Percy said skeptically.

Vipera grinned. "No."

Three

"What's all this? We hardly ever get any visitors at our tower."

Vipera shoved past the tall, thin man in a blue cloak, while Percy, Aresto, Kai, and Archer stayed behind. "This is urgent. We've heard that a chimera is in the area. You need to drive it off."

"Ma'am, I believe you are mistaken. Plus, even if it were true, our tower has incredible defenses. We'd be fine against a single chimera."

"Not this one," Vipera said. "This is the leader of the chimeras down at Gados. The strongest one. The only way to be safe is to kill it."

"We're not soldiers," the man said indignantly.

"But you're knights, aren't you?" Vipera said. "Maybe this will finally get your organization the recognition you want from the Interstellar Association."

That seemed to win the man over. "Fine. Do you have any idea where the chimera is right now?"

Vipera pointed down the valley to where Cyclone was hiding, ready to set the chimera free.

"All forces!" the man shouted inside the tower. "Get your mounts! We have a threat to the tower!"

Within minutes, they had set off down the valley, every one of them – even Vipera, Percy, Aresto, and the others – riding a hippogriff.

Vipera was up front, giving directions to the tall man, but she flew off to the side, out of his earshot, after a few minutes. Percy heard her tell Cyclone to release the chimera.

Sure enough, when she rejoined the group, a large beast flew out of one of the crevices to face the group. It had the forequarters of a lion, the wings and tail of a dragon, and the hindquarters of a goat – plus the heads of all three.

The dragon head immediately started aggressively breathing fire, and the chimera flew forwards into the middle of the group and started slashing.

The most surprising part was when the goat head opened its mouth and breathed out a beam of lightning.

Now Percy realized why Cyclone had brought a chimera – it was a combination of animals, with an added special power.

"Focus on driving it away!" Vipera shouted. "Killing it will prove hard, driving it out of the valley should be much easier."

The chimera expertly dodged every attack the knights threw at it, although Percy did notice that it was slowly being pushed to the edge of the canyon.

"We have a problem!!" one of the knights said, and Percy turned to see what she was talking about. His eyes widened in shock.

Their plan had succeeded, but instead of one griffin hunting them, a giant flock of them was flying at top speed towards them.

"RETREAT!!" the tall man yelled, and the hippogriffs all turned, flying back to the tower.

Percy tried to steer his mount towards the griffins, but it was too busy fleeing for its life.

"We'll have to levitate," Cyclone's voice said through Percy's earpiece. "I know it's dangerous, but we have no other option."

But Percy saw one other option. It was also dangerous, but he really didn't want to fly alone into the group of griffins. So he flew straight towards the chimera and jumped.

He barely managed to land on the chimera's furry back, but it was right as the beast was turning, and the red leathery wing tipped him back to a more stable position.

It took a moment for the chimera to realize that there was someone on its back, and when it did, it thrashed around, indifferent to the places it was shooting fire. Several of the griffins took critical injuries, diving down to safety. Several more were killed on the spot.

"Cyclone! Control your chimera!" Vipera shouted. "It's hurting all the beasts we need!"

"I'm trying!" came Cyclone's reply. "But it seems to have gone berserk now that someone's on its back. Plus, we only need *one* griffin."

One of the griffins made a particularly brutal attack against the chimera's wing, causing it to spiral downwards out of control right towards the place Cyclone and the others were.

"Cyclone! Throw me the nets!" Percy shouted. "I'm gonna try to fly back up and catch the griffin!"

For a moment, Percy thought nothing would happen. But then a large bundle of what must have been thirty nets landed on the chimera's back. Percy grabbed it so it wouldn't fall off.

Unfortunately, he wasn't able to fly back up. At the least, he was able to slow his descent, but the griffins had won and they knew it.

Just as the chimera was about to crash into the rocky ground, a woman with jet-black hair jumped from a crevice in the canyon wall and landed next to Percy.

"Who are you?" Percy said.

The woman glared at him. "Quiet. Let me focus."

She stretched out her hand and touched one of the dragon head's horns. Instantly, a yellow-green light began to glow from her hand all the way to the chimera's right wing, and the wound began to heal.

The chimera realized that it was all right, and it flew straight up towards the griffins, roaring in fury. Percy tried to stand up as best he could, and he wrapped a net around the griffin that had just flown by, wrapping his leg around the chimera's body to keep him from flying off.

The griffin immediately ripped right through the net and kept on flying.

Percy tried the same tactic with a different griffin, with the same result.

"Don't they say that the definition of insanity is trying the same thing over and over and expecting a different result?" the woman said.

"Three things," Percy said. "One – I'm pretty sure *nobody* says that, two – you are absolutely no help at all, and three – who even *are* you?"

"My name's Vera. I'm one of the people Vipera rounded up to help with this experiment, and I'm a Healer. And without me, you would have crashed. I think that counts as help."

"Fine, whatever – can you hold these and try to catch a griffin?" Percy handed her the nets.

She frowned. "Have you learned nothing? Obviously we need to try something different."

"Trust me, I've got a plan. You can steer the chimera better than I can, right?"

"I'm pretty sure everyone could."

Percy ignored the insult. "Everyone who's down below, can you hear me?"

A chorus of "yes" came through Percy's earpiece.

"Perfect. I need all of you to use your telekinesis to make the chimera stop in its tracks when I say. Vera, I need you to focus on catching the griffin."

Vera nodded.

"Get ready... NOW!"

Vera threw a net around a particularly large griffin at the same time Percy shot a beam of electricity at the net. The griffin instantly stopped moving for fear of being shocked, and Percy felt the chimera jerk backwards as it froze too.

"Add as many nets as you can!" Percy shouted at Vera.

Without question, Vera put on net after net until Percy could barely see the griffin under all the mesh.

"I'm gonna remove the electricity," Percy said. "The griffin will probably start destroying the nets as soon as I do, so I need all of you to bring the chimera down to where you all are."

"Go ahead," Cyclone said.

Percy stretched out his hand, thinking of all the times he had done the exact same thing during his training. Then he sucked the electricity back into his arm and shot it out in the sky.

Sure enough, the griffin instantly started trying to claw through the nets, but Cyclone and the others stayed true to their word, and Percy had to hold on with everything he had to keep from flying off.

The chimera had enough strength to control its landing, and as soon as it touched down, everybody rushed over and clipped four dark orange metal bracelets on the griffin's legs.

"These will keep the griffin from flying off," Cyclone explained as he put the same bands on the chimera.

"Also, WHAT WERE YOU THINKING?" Aresto shouted as Percy slid off the oblivious griffin. "Flying on an out-of-control beast into a horde of vicious griffins? That was insane!"

Percy smiled. "I'm just glad it worked. I honestly had no idea if it would. Who's that over there, by the way?"

Everyone turned to where a woman made completely out of fire was standing in the far corner of the cavern.

"This is Selene, our fire demon strategist," Cyclone said. "She's the other person Vipera recruited. With her, we have thirteen – which definitely should be enough. Should we all agree to meet tomorrow at my office? We can discuss next steps about the phoenix from there."

"That soon?" Aria said.

"Of course. I fear the Council is already beginning to suspect that I am up to something. The quicker we can get this done, the better. My office, nine o'clock."

Four

Percy stared out of the window of his room.

His house was on the very edge of civilization, so he got a gorgeous view from his window – giant pink hills, mountains on the horizon, at least three clear lakes in sight – which made him think...

"Aresto? Do you really think what we're doing is the right thing?"

Aresto frowned. "What do you mean?"

"I don't know, it's just... I mean, look out at the countryside. The Forgotten World is already beautiful. Is human intervention really necessary?"

Aresto sat down next to him. "I think you're biased. Unintentionally, of course, but you've always grown up with this view. We both have. We haven't seen the less beautiful parts of the Forgotten World – the parts that need help."

"I guess, but isn't there another way? Capturing these creatures and forcing them to combine just seems... wrong."

"We're not doing anything to harm them. They'll still be just as alive and well as they are now. They'll just be together."

"Are you sure? Correct me if I'm wrong, but Cyclone still hasn't told us *how* we're going to combine them."

"Why bother telling us that now when we're only a third of the way to getting there? We just have to trust that he knows what he's doing."

"But that's the problem. I *don't* trust him."

Aresto sighed. "Well, I'm following through with his plan. It's our best chance."

Percy did not expect his Saturday to start with someone slamming him against a wall, nor to recognize the slick blonde hair and pointed ears as that of his nephew.

"Walker? What are you doing?"

"I should ask you the same thing," Walker growled. "I know you and Aresto are up to something, I know you're working with Cyclone, and I know *why* you're doing it. Oh, and I know it's illegal too."

"You have no proof," Percy said.

"Funny how you say that instead of denying my accusation. And I don't need proof yet. I only need to continue my investigation. But as a Councilor, I need to report this as soon as I learn more."

"What investigation is this?" Percy asked.

Walker smiled. "One that you have no need to know anything else about. Just know that I have ways of finding out what you're up to."

"Did the Council give you the assignment of spying on me, or are you doing it by yourself?"

Walker's smile faltered. "That is something you do not need to know. But I would stop now if I were you. This is dangerous territory you're in, Percy."

"I'm glad you all were able to make it again," Cyclone said. "Especially you, Selene. You will be invaluable during these next steps."

"Getting the phoenix?" Selene asked. "What's our plan for that?"

"This one was a little trickier," Cyclone admitted. "But I've figured it out. I found a hidden phoenix nesting spot on the planet Volcania. That's where you're from, isn't it, Selene?"

"It is... but I don't see how I could help – I've never heard of any phoenixes on that planet."

"You would help more than any of us. All we know is where it is. You know the best ways to get there, spots to avoid

– all the important things. We will, however, need a lot more preparation than we had for the griffin. As a fire elemental, a phoenix will prove extremely difficult to capture. But with a fire demon and a Pyrokinetic on our team, we can do it. Aresto and Selene, I need you to accompany me to Volcania tomorrow to scope out the area. We'll continue forming the plan from there. Percy, can you take everyone else to your family's element training room?"

"Sure – should we just focus on fire?"

"Yes. Having at least some control over fire will be essential. Aresto and Selene – and Vipera, you'd better come with me too. We'll hold a meeting when we return."

Percy didn't know what to expect when everyone began the fiery obstacle courses, but they finished them quicker than he expected. Within two hours, they were doing things that Percy himself might find challenging.

The whole time, he couldn't help thinking about what Aresto was doing at Volcania.

Finally, Selene arrived at the training room, all by herself.

"Where's Aresto?" Percy asked.

"He's still with Cyclone and Vipera. They wanted to test something out."

"What'd you decide on with the plan?" Silas said.

Selene smiled. "Turns out, all the phoenixes on Volcania are dead. So they're planning something with Aresto's pyro-whatever stuff to raise a phoenix from the ashes. I think that's how it works?"

"It is," Bismarck said. "Whenever a phoenix dies, a new one is born – so if they can force the ashes to create a new phoenix, it should be that much easier."

"Am I the only one who thinks that this plan is… unnecessary?" Archer said. "I mean, the Forgotten World isn't perfect, but human intervention can't be the best plan."

Percy sighed. "I agree. It seemed like a good step at first, but now that I really think about it, the chances of it actually helping are very slim. Aresto supports it completely, though."

"So should we follow through with it?" Aria said. "Or should we stop?"

"Not only should we stop, we might need to take active preparations to stop *them*," Percy said. "But I say let's see what they do with the phoenix first."

No one disagreed.

Five

Volcania was *hot*.

Giant rivers of lava flowed through the rough land, and the sky was a cloudy red. Percy watched Aresto eagerly discuss the plan again with Cyclone and Vipera, while he trailed behind.

Percy wasn't supposed to have come, but Aresto had convinced Cyclone that Percy's mastery of the elements would serve them well, and Cyclone had allowed it. So now Percy had his chance to stop them.

But how? He didn't even know what the plan was.

The feathers that normally transported people from planet to planet were trackable by the Council, so Cyclone opted to use a Teleporter.

Cyclone held up his hand. "This spot will do. Aresto, Percy, please go scout out the surrounding area. Make sure we are alone."

Aresto and Percy jogged down the hill.

"You're really following through with this?" Percy asked once they were out of Cyclone's earshot.

"Of course. I've made my position clear. And if you want to keep helping, you need to make up your mind."

Percy sighed. "I think I already have."

"You're not gonna follow through with it."

It wasn't a question, but Percy nodded anyway.

"You realize that this is the best option? Something needs to be done."

"No it doesn't," Percy said. "The Forgotten World isn't perfect, but nothing is. And compared to so many other places, the Forgotten World is one of the better ones."

"But what if we could make it perfect?" Aresto said. "Wouldn't that be so much better?"

"Not when Cyclone's the one leading the experiment. He's power-hungry, Aresto. His idea for a perfect world is one where he's in charge. One where there is no Council."

"The Councilors don't know what they're doing anyway. Wouldn't a new leader be better?"

"It would if it wasn't Cyclone."

"Look, the Forgotten World may not be at its worst *now*, but I want to purify it *permanantly.* If it truly is not so bad, I want to make it so that it won't be that bad a thousand years from now."

"But it *won't.* It's not getting any worse."

"I don't want to fight you, Percy, but I *am* going to finish this experiment."

"You'll be the only one. Every single other person that we recruited – even Selene and Vera – are on my side here."

"So you won't let me finish this?"

"Not a chance."

Aresto said nothing for a moment, then out of nowhere, with a flaming fist, he lunged towards Percy. Percy dodged, but only barely.

Aresto dove out of the way as Percy hurled a ball of lightning towards him. The lightning instead slammed into the rocks behind him, dispersing once it made contact.

Percy levitated straight upwards, boosting his flight with a burst of air. Once he was out of the range of a melee attack, he hurled three large beams of light at Aresto. Spinning around and lighting his fists, Aresto deflected all three beams, which rebounded away from the fight.

"We won't get anywhere like this, Percy," Aresto called out. "We both have extreme control over every element. Neither of us is stronger than the other."

Percy smiled. "You're forgetting one thing. Electricity isn't one of the elements. And *I* have control over that."

A dark, wheezy voice – all too familiar at this point – spoke. "And *he* has *me*."

Percy didn't register that Cyclone had attacked him until he fell to the ground, convulsing violently from the electricity flowing through his body.

Cyclone was an Electrokinetic too?

The only thing he saw was Cyclone's chimera lowering its head, allowing Aresto to climb on, before everything went black.

The chimera flew over what must have been at least five raging rivers of lava before it landed where Vipera was waiting.

"Aresto, we're counting on you to get us started," Cyclone said. "We just need a tiny spark to start the flame. That's all it takes."

Aresto took a deep breath before a small fire appeared on his palm.

"Now everybody take each other's hands. We're going to project the fire upwards. Concentrate with everything you have... NOW!"

Aresto grasped Cyclone's hand, and the fire spread around the three of them, before shooting towards the sky.

Even as a Pyrokinetic, Aresto could feel his whole body heating up and he didn't know how much longer he could last.

But then a shape formed in the flames.

And out flew a giant dark red bird with flaming feathers.

The fire disappeared, and Aresto collapsed to the ground, closely followed by Vipera. Cyclone held his ground, though, pulling the dark orange bands out of his cloak and levitating upwards.

Just as he was about to reach the bird, it swerved out of the way, and he caught a glimpse of the person riding it.

"You think you can get rid of me that easily??" Percy shouted. "You think you'll capture the phoenix?"

"He's controlling it," Cyclone muttered. "How is he controlling it?"

"How did you get back up?" Vipera said, at the same moment Cyclone threw a lightning bolt at Percy.

Percy stretched out his hand and absorbed the lightning, shooting it back up in the sky. "Just like that. I'll admit, it was a bit difficult, given the amount of electricity that was in my body, but I didn't train with all the elements for nothing."

"How are you controlling the phoenix?" Cyclone said.

"You of all people should know this," Percy said. "A phoenix inherently trusts the first person who rides it. So I really must thank you for using a newly born one – you've made *my* job that much easier."

Cyclone gritted his teeth and pressed two fingers to his earpiece. "I need Percy out of my way! Call Gavin!"

"I'm already here," said a voice from behind Percy.

He spun around to see a young man with long unnaturally blue hair and clothes so casual, it was like he wasn't planning on fighting. *When had he gotten on the phoenix?*

Percy lunged for Gavin, but in a fraction of a second, Gavin was behind him. He shot a bolt of lightning behind him, but Gavin wasn't there anymore, instead on one of the phoenix's wings.

Gavin jumped in front of Percy, but within three seconds, was behind him. Percy then realized what was going on – Gavin was a Teleporter.

He felt Gavin's hands on his head and tried to yank them off, but his arms dropped to his sides. His eyelids drooped. He felt himself going limp. Not only that, all his emotions had left him.

He couldn't feel.

Couldn't think.

Could barely see or hear.

Everything was gray and fuzzy.

And then the world sharpened into focus, and he felt himself falling. The phoenix got smaller and smaller, and then everything went black as he slammed into the ground.

He woke up in his bedroom, where everyone was crowded around him.

"What happened?" he groaned, trying to sit up.

"You fell off the phoenix," Kai Andersen answered. "It's a miracle you're alive. You didn't even try to levitate. It looked like you were already unconscious. Selene arrived just in time to rescue you and get you out of there."

"That's not what I meant," he said, but the grim looks everyone else was exchanging told him what he wanted to know.

"They got the phoenix," Selene said.

"You're the leader," said Archer. "What do we do?"

Percy finally managed to sit up, propping his head against his pillow. "It's time to begin preparations to stop them. Even if we lose, it's not over until one of us wins."

Percy and Aresto will return in

Part 2

Schubert's 8th Symphony

Tabitha Miles

Chapter 1

Reflecting on the past year of my life sends a cold shiver through my wounded spine, causing excruciating pain in my exhausted body. The freezing air seemed to stretch the lonely quiet night until morning, making it feel as if the hours would never pass, neither growing in warmth nor comfort. My hand reached out to the end of the table in front of me, barely brushing the polished wood. I forced what energy I had left into my frostbitten fingers, closing it on the burned and tattered letter. I ripped the envelope open with purpose of what comes next. My shaking hands bearing the weight of paper, reaching and grasping the thin sheets. Words filled pages of desperate letters and calls for help, but one caught my eye, the letters seeming to flash before my eyes in a way like no other. The short choppy sentences worried my confused mind. I pushed the air out of my lungs, breathing, before I reached for the last piece of paper.

The letter finishes.

The wind blew my tent door open, but I couldn't force myself to close it. My eye, exposed to the dawn light, bled wet tears that streamed down my dirty face. My shoulders shook with the beat of my dreaded life. The crowded space inside wasn't much of anything, but going home wasn't an option. It was never an option after that night I got picked for the war.

\#

Walking down the main street of Edinburgh was my favorite thing, especially when the bus sped by gusting wind my way, and every girl flashed me her prettiest smile, but today was different. I was pacing through the streets. With haste and purpose but really I felt like peeing my pants. My mom was probably freaking out in our small kitchen. I was trying to be home as fast as I could after work but traffic and my boss seemed to hate me today, so I ran home, trying to make up for the lost time.

Not a good idea. I ended up running all the way home and ripped a hole through my brand-new shirt when I tripped and literally fell on my face, my mom was going to be so happy, not really.

I got home a lot later than I usually did but hoped my charm and sometimes kindness would work magic with my mom tonight.

It did not.

I entered the barely lit house, hoping to be unnoticed but after I got past the abandoned porch and opened the main house door, I was busted. Both my parents were waiting for me to finally come home, which was a very very rare occurrence. Their heads didn't turn, they didn't even move any muscle in their body. My mom sat on her rocking chair knitting a blanket for my younger brother. He was close to death from the flu, my mom wanted to keep him at home but father made sure he had to go to the hospital, and get some help, but guess who's paying for it, you're reading about him. Me. Yay. My mother made something for him every other day, hoping something can save him. My father and I both knew he wouldn't make it, but we would never tell him that. My father was cleaning our few dishes in a bucket next to our faucet, kneeling on his bad knee. I walked past them both almost sprinting to my room, I reached for the handle but,

"Where do you think you're going, Tation Colin?"

I spun around towards the voice of my mother and walked back into our main room,

"To sleep?"

"Do you really think we were going to let you go to bed without speaking to us first?" My father sounded nice, but the kindness in his voice was so forced anyone could tell he was faking it.

"Of course not, Father." I returned the same tone, which I was immediately regretting. My father put the last plate to dry on our only dish towel without any holes, we rarely used that one.

My parents shared a look before turning to me. "What were the results?"

I knew they were talking about the draft, but playing dumb was the only option, so I said nothing.

"What results?" My father stared at me with disgust and hatred, I knew I messed up. He grabbed the soaking plate and threw it against the wall of one of the only windows in our house, sending pieces of sharp broken glass and wet water droplets against my bare skin, and my mother's.

My mother shrank against the force of the deep cuts, but was too scared to make any sort of sound. She shivered in the corner, fearing what move my father would make next. I, on the other hand, did not care. My father was drunk and usually was, so why would it make a difference if he broke one of his plates that he paid for. Why should I care that he hates my family and tortures my mother? Why should I care if my little brother tells all his friends he doesn't have a father? Life may be better without him, but he's here, living and somehow surviving.

My father yelled at me the whole rest of the night, cursing my name and calling my mother a witch. I tried to go to sleep but he was at my door the whole night, banging and crying screaming I was the worst. He finally gave up after I told him that we were out of whisky, and then he threw a tantrum, and then he yelled at my mom for an hour, but once she's out she won't wake up until morning. After his hissyfit and ripping the small shards of glass out of his scrubby face, he passed out.

The sun rose and I still was yet to crack and tell my parents, it's not that I didn't want them to know or that I was disappointed or sad necessarily, just that I didn't know how I was supposed to feel. I headed out the door after a disappointing breakfast of an apple and oatmeal. I saved the orange for my little brother, whose name is Covet by the way. I searched my pocket for any money left to see if I could take the bus, of course there was a shocking amount of nothing. I had to run half the way so I wasn't late. I loved walking past the money lake, especially in the morning with the bright big beam reflecting the somewhat murky water and into the smallish desert things, no one knows really what.

The trail was hardly used so the path was overgrown with lovely daisies and small sunflowers, scenting it with the sweetness of sugar and never going away, until winter. I was rounding the corner of Jinx's coffee shop when I heard the click of her tiny heels hitting the uneven pavement. The over strong smell of sweet artificial flavor that hits you if you are within ten feet of her. You can see her shiny jewelry from a country away, it blinds you if you stare too long.

Emily Smith, every girl wanted to be her, and every boy wanted to marry her. She was faker than a cigar, looking so pretty and nice on the outside and everyone wants to have one, but is as nasty as tar. I never talked to her, although she followed me like a puppy. I always either ignored her or just walked away from her sly smile and petty face. I hated her more than my father, which was saying something.

I walked down 5th street straight to Anvil and Hammer, my home basically, I liked the people there more anyways, so it made sense. I checked the clock above the Jinx's coffee shop, seven twenty, but the clock ran twenty minutes ahead. So he had fifteen minutes to get to work, he had to be there at seven twenty, but the boss liked it better if I was five minutes early, so I had time.

I took somewhat of a short cut through downtown and 8th alleyways. But sometimes sketchy Chris and freaky Toby come down, and don't for the love of God please don't come across them, and that's what I stay away from them, for my mother's sake and my own. I cut through main street traffic towards Chloe's fabric shop. I liked watching Chloe study the perfect fabric falling into a young child or unkind mother. Her face scrunches against her arched eyebrow, her cute flat lips pressed together as her eyes bulge from her small sockets. She looked angry and sad but determined to get that fabric away from this monster. I watched her across the street near the pony newspaper, Scott would be there, I ran for reasons unknown and unneeded, but beautiful as they were. I stopped inches from getting impaled by some idiot who obviously couldn't see.

"YO! Slow the roll dude I need some space to breathe and not die!" I said. The dude looked up shocked by being called out by literally anyone. I flashed his bright green unnatural eyes back and forth across the street and back towards the sweating and natural so handsome me. He bit his lip not needing to watch the traffic apparently and sprinted across the busy dirt road and shoved his covered and somehow very dusty cart of who knows what. I shook myself, sending the beads of sweat across and turning the brown first to one shade darker of course. I continued my battle cry towards the front door of the newspaper shop hoping Scott could somehow save me from a mid-life crisis. I flung the cracked and tattered chipping green front door hitting the wall next to it, and I would probably be yelled at by Saucy, Scotts boss, but who cares, he's a grump and somehow very fit. What he gains in muscles, he loses in hair. I scanned the front room of the shop with my light brown eyes, looking for my best bud and hoping he was here. He was sitting in the baby blue foot rest, don't ask me why, he's a weird dude. He was reading a version of Little Red Riding Hood. I huffed myself over to the chair next to him, being a dramatic baby, so he got my point. He returned the favor by rolling his eyes to glare at me.

"Have you told them?" Scott asked?

"No, but I think they already know, and when I leave they *will* know, especially since it's today. I don't want to go, but really there's nothing I can do. You're so lucky, staying with Stacy must be nice." I said, trying to stay in the conversation but drifting through the reactions of my family once they knew. Scott opened his mouth wanting to say something but it slammed shut when the horn blared through the small downtown, I ran out not wanting to say goodbye, saying goodbye is bad luck obviously. I jumped on the small military bus, not wanting to look back, thinking I will see this place, my family, and my friends. Man how wrong I was.

Chapter 2

I went through basic training in a flash, nothing happened. I mean I became ten times more ripped, but really nothing happened. Basic training went like this, worked out, shot some dummies, slept, ate, and repeated. I didn't sleep much. Basic training left me numb, but I jumped into AIT (advanced individual training) for infantry. Honestly if you asked me what that is, infantry, I genuinely don't know. Scott scrambled through it a bit but it was going straight through one ear and out the other. Part of my beautiful gentle soul died through that long frustrating twelve weeks. That's the first time I cried in the first time since my pet snake got killed by a rake, by my father. That also was when I was twelve, I'm eighteen now. The night I sobbed, shaking with defeat, is the night I left for First Station Unit training.

AIT wasn't enough preparation for First Unit training. It wasn't physically challenging, mentally I died inside. We worked for hours being yelled at, sweared at, and so much more. I am used to it but having someone almost kill you and then

SCHUBERT'S 8TH SYMPHONY

say, "hey good job not letting me kill you." is a little bit of a different story. I also just didn't like the people here and nobody liked me, glad it was mutual. I couldn't even get up in the morning, because of my fear of truly closing my eyes without completely passing out. I can hear you laughing at me, but listen. Hearing bombing screaming war talk death threats isn't the most idle way to fall asleep. And I'm pretty sure some of the soldiers were making bets on how I would die. Little did they know breaking me, never works, it only changes me.

I left the small drafty

281

Also Available at DrabaticPress.com:

Twelve Upon a Time is a delightful collection of fairy tales, all original, from the author that brought you the book you're holding in your hands. Fifteen whimsical stories (the author can't count) of princesses, wizards, and children of all ages. From the modern to the traditional, here are perfect read-aloud tales that will enchant children and adults alike.

Like Nancy Drew? Wish there were another, maybe just *slightly* more adventurous lady detective out there solving

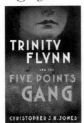

crimes? Maybe, say, in New York? In the speakeasy/jazz era of the 1920s? Meet Trinity Flynn, two parts Nancy Drew, one part Agent Peggy Carter, with a quart bottle of Amelia Earhart thrown in. She's a college student in the big city

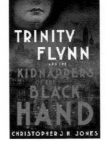

Roaring 20s—and she's up to her neck in trouble. Whether it's saving her roommate and solving a gang murder in *Trinity Flynn and the Five Points Gang* or going undercover to rescue a kidnapped five-year-old in *Trinity Flynn and the Kidnappers of the Black Hand*, we guarantee Trinity Flynn is the girl for you.

Available at DrabaticPress.com

Made in the USA
Columbia, SC
11 July 2024

7dcf7a85-5d03-40a7-bd36-d18402cde78fR01